"I don't feel guilty f[ ]
with sobs. "I'm guilty b[ ]
up her life *unknowingly* for me. And I haven't been able to mourn
her. I didn't attend her funeral, and I haven't cried, and—"

"You're crying right now," Audrie interrupted, trying to smile.

Nolia's words became unintelligible as she wept harder, holding onto Audrie as if she was all that she had left. Audrie gripped her tightly because she was afraid that she was. That Nolia would never have anyone else love her as much as she or Corinne did.

Audrie hadn't realized that she'd begun to cry as well until Nolia wiped one of her tears from her cheek.

"How selfish of me," she mumbled. "To act like my problems are the only ones that matter when you're facing loss too. Your brother's dead, and he may have always hated me, but he loved you in his cruel way."

Audrie choked back a sob of her own. "Alaric?" she said. "He didn't hate you, he loved you in his own way too. I heard him say so, right before I..."

But she was unable to continue, and Nolia held her now as her own bawling filled the room. She wanted to tell Nolia that Alaric hadn't wanted her to die after the Competition. That he'd later begged Audrie to take Nolia away so that they wouldn't be forced to kill her. She wanted Nolia to know what Katrine had said about Alaric when she'd been a baby.

Yet as these thoughts swirled around her mind, Audrie knew that there was only one thing that she *had* to say.

"I killed him."

Nolia's eyes widened, pulling away in shock. "What?"

"I killed Alaric." Audrie was hardly able to see through her tears. "To save you. I'm sorry, I'm so sorry. I wanted to kill Elias, but my plan was ruined by the coronation and your sudden appearance. I didn't have a choice. I promise I didn't have a choice. I swear I—"

Nolia enveloped her in her arms again. "It's alright," she whispered. "It's going to be alright, Audrie."

6

Nolia

THE SUN HAD not yet risen when Yadira shook Nolia awake. She'd tried to speak, but the teenage queen had only shook her head before motioning towards Audrie's sleeping form in the bed next to her. It'd taken hours for both of them to drift off despite hardly speaking after Audrie admitted to Alaric's murder.

Nolia wasn't sure how to feel about it, but she did know that no one else could find out. Especially not Audrie's family.

Yadira helped Nolia into what she thought was the queenliest piece of clothing in her wardrobe. It was a white gown with a tight lace bodice and ruffled skirt that fell down to Nolia's feet. There were pearls stitched in small perfect lines on the hem of each ruffle.

"Your Majesty needs a crown," Yadira said quietly.

Nolia barely heard her, too busy avoiding looking at her mother's gowns hanging on the racks around her. Or on her shoes organized neatly in a wall-to-floor cupboard. Or on her makeup and hair tools that sat on the vanity to her right. She stared at her reflection instead, in the large three panel mirror.

"Your Majesty?"

Nolia shifted her gaze to Yadira in the mirror. "I don't have a crown, you know I wasn't allowed to wear one until I'm married."

"But you're queen," Yadira said. "You can't wait to be married to start looking like what you are."

Nolia grimaced. *Katrine rarely wore one,* she wanted to argue. But now wasn't the time for comparisons, even if all she'd ever wanted was to be as good of a queen as her mother had been. She knew in her heart that after everything that had happened, Nolia needed to be better than Katrine. She needed to rid Icaria of its remaining rebels, and she needed allies in order to do that.

Allies that needed to be able to see her as queen, instead of the inexperienced teenage girl she was.

"Do you see where she kept them?" Nolia quickly scanned the room before realizing that the large chandelier hanging over her head was making the cupboard to the right of the vanity twinkle. They were organized as nicely as the shoes, except the headwear had been placed on soft cushioning.

"Never mind," Nolia mumbled, stepping carefully off the platform in front of the mirror to follow Yadira, who'd already skipped over.

"There's so many options," she said breathlessly. She seemed tempted to run her fingers over all of them. "What about that one?" She pointed to a large topaz tiara that Nolia had seen Katrine wear multiple times. "Or perhaps an amethyst one?" Yadira suggested, pointing to the many in the collection. "Purple is the Icarian royal color so—"

"I'm wearing pearls," Nolia interrupted. "I'd like to wear something with pearls on it."

Yadira sighed. "Must you always wear white?"

"Yes," Nolia said with a shrug. "I look good in white."

• • •

The map room was where Nolia was supposed to meet with Katrine's council. It was yet another room that she'd never been allowed inside of, but had passed the wooden doors plenty of times when going or leaving the throne room as they were down the hall from one another.

When the guards opened the doors for her, Nolia was surprised to already find the five members of the queen's council inside, waiting for her on their knees with their heads bowed.

"My queen."

Nolia followed the voice, smiling shyly. "Uncle Thiodore."

Despite his place on Katrine's council and frequent attendance at court as Katrine's favorite brother, he and Nolia never spent time together. They rarely had things to talk about when they did, but he was fond of her. Growing up, most of her toys had been gifts from him, and now that she was older, she occasionally received a book or a piece of jewelry from him.

Now her uncle was grinning at her, his royal blue eyes sparkling with encouragement.

"Thank you for being here," Nolia told her mother's council. "Please sit with me."

She walked past them to the chair she knew was meant for her. It was the largest one, with a velvet purple cushion similar to the queen's throne, and at the head of the stone table. The room was otherwise empty, the only decoration being the different maps hanging on every open piece of wall that the two windows behind the queen's chair didn't take up. However, none were as extravagant as the map of Icaria that had been expertly and painstakingly painted on the table to get every single detail of the queendom correctly.

The members stood, and Thiodore rushed to Nolia's chair so that he could push it in for her. She smiled her gratitude as he went to his own seat across from hers, likely meant to be a place of honor.

"We're glad to be here," Alexie said from her place on Nolia's right. She'd always been one of the army commanders that Nolia liked to receive combat lessons from, but she favored the red head all the more now since she'd helped Nolia after Elias' attempted takeover.

Next to her was Lady Gristola, nodding her agreement. She was a tall woman with rosy skin, black hair, and small hazel eyes. She and Katrine had been friends growing up, but Nolia wouldn't have considered them best friends.

"We're here to help you fix what Elias has done."

Nolia turned towards the new voice, gratitude on the tip of her tongue before pausing.

52

Lady Rianne stared back at her, nervously. She was the youngest member of Katrine's council and its newest member, but Nolia had met her before. Nolia had acknowledged that Rianne had lovely black hair, warm brown eyes, and umber skin, but hadn't paid any attention to her appearance otherwise. Now all Nolia could see was the resemblance to Jibril, Mikael's father.

Rianne nodded once, almost as if she knew what Nolia was thinking.

Why didn't Mikael tell me that one of his many sisters was on my mother's council? Nolia wondered. It certainly seemed like the sort of thing he should have mentioned.

"I believe that we should first discuss the matter of your coronation."

Nolia managed to tear her gaze away from Rianne to the last member of her mother's council: Sir Marvin. He sat next to Rianne, his light blue eyes squinting at Nolia behind his thick spectacles. Marvin was the sole member of the council that Katrine hadn't appointed, as he was the only member from Queen Isiris' council that she'd never replaced. Out of everyone on the council, Marvin was who Nolia knew best, as he'd been her history tutor. She wondered now if her new appointment as queen meant that those lessons would come to an end.

"I second the topic of Her Majesty's coronation," Rianne agreed.

Nolia cleared her throat awkwardly when the council turned towards her expectantly. Did they not realize that she had no idea how these meetings were conducted?

"Why do we need to discuss my coronation so soon after my mother's death?" Nolia asked. "I know they take planning, but the queendom needs time to mourn. The matter of Elias' inevitable execution is something we can do now."

"We can't, Your High—Majesty," Marvin said, placing his palms on the table. "Only a crowned monarch can order an execution."

Nolia blinked. "Then how was my father trying to execute me when he hadn't been crowned?"

"I wouldn't say he's the best example, considering he was a usurper," Alexie reminded her gently.

"He also would have been crowned if you hadn't stopped the coronation," Rianne said, looking impressed.

"By breaking the crown of Icaria," Marvin added, sounding very unimpressed.

"A new one can be made, can't it?" Nolia answered, barely stopping herself from crossing her arms. She had a feeling it would make her look like a toddler throwing a tantrum.

"That crown is made of Icarian gold," Marvin told her. "We never had much to begin with, and we have less now." His eyes lost focus as they tended to during his history lessons. "It's the same case with the jewels. We have plenty of diamonds, but it's been years since a ruby, emerald, or sapphire has appeared in our mines."

"The jewels are intact," Gristola spoke up. "I examined them late last night, and they're in perfect condition. All we need is enough Icarian gold to make the base of the crown."

Marvin shook his head, his eyes shifting in Gristola's direction, but still not quite seeing her. "It would take years to mine the amount we need."

"Perhaps we don't have to mine for it."

Everyone turned to Thiodore. The prince fiddled with a pendant in his hands, not looking up as he continued, "There's more Icarian gold in existence than you may think, *especially* within the palaces."

Thiodore lifted his pendant which Nolia could see now was a compass, a shade of gold deeper than the one that came from the mainland, marking it as the Icarian kind. "This is an example, an heirloom we've had in the family for generations made of Icarian gold. I'd gladly give it up, however, to be melted down to build a new crown for Nolia."

Nolia was touched by his offer and smiled brightly at him, but before she could speak, Rianne did.

"That won't be enough to make a crown," she said. "We'd need *many* pendants."

"I know of a large enough piece of Icarian gold we could use," Nolia said as she remembered the dark coloring of the mirror over Katrine's fireplace. "It would be more than enough to make a crown."

"Perhaps we should look for a statue or something that will make just enough for a crown?" Gristola suggested. "Choosing to destroy priceless royal items should be done with care."

"I'm sure there's something that'll melt down into the exact amount needed for a crown," Alexie agreed.

"Except that our welders may need extra gold in case of any mistakes," Rianne pointed out.

"Our welders likely won't have the expertise to recreate such a special crown, especially quickly," Marvin said. "Nonetheless, shall we leave it to a vote?"

"I'm *offering* what item to use," Nolia quickly announced before anyone else could speak. "So why can't we use it instead of wasting time searching for Icarian gold elsewhere?"

The council members glanced at one another.

"So you won't allow us to vote?" Gristola asked. "You've decided yourself, Your Majesty?"

Nolia could hear the disapproval in her tone, and she wasn't certain how to respond to it. A part of her wanted to lash out, but the other part was afraid. Was she doing something wrong by not allowing them to vote? Was this not the way a council meeting was supposed to go?

"Nolia is queen, and she can do whatever she likes," Thiodore came to her rescue. "She doesn't have to run the council the same way Katrine did."

Gristola didn't seem to agree, but Nolia smiled again at her uncle, suddenly grateful that Katrine had appointed him to her council. Just as Thiodore had always been on Katrine's side, he would always be on Nolia's.

"So it's decided." Nolia sat up straighter. "We'll have it melted down, and possibly have a new crown by the end of the week."

"Which leads us to the details regarding your coronation," Alexie said after a moment of silence.

"And the execution that will follow," Rianne added. "Will you execute your father immediately following your crowning?"

"It will not simply be her father," Gristola said. "His other followers will need to be punished too, like his mistress and her family."

"Audrie will *not* die." The words came out with such viciousness that it even surprised Nolia. "She's not Elias' daughter, and Cecily and Josip have already shown they're willing to cooperate with me."

"We cannot simply allow them to live," Gristola objected. "They participated in a coup to overthrow your mother and kill you. Cecily went as far as marrying Elias to—"

"Yes, actually I'd like to discuss that," Nolia interrupted. "Elias claimed that the council annulled Cecily and Josip's marriage."

"That was his false council," Rianne told her. "The same ones who arranged the betrothal between Alaric and Katiana."

Nolia frowned. "Who's Katiana?"

The council glanced at one another again.

"You've been a bit too busy to hear the wonderful news, what with taking your throne back and all," Thiodore said, staring at the other members pointedly. "Your Uncle Kristopher's new wife gave birth to a little girl. She went into labor the day of the maze trial. They named her Katiana."

A new cousin, was Nolia's first thought, and it brought her some joy. Especially since the only cousins she'd had before were boys. They'd also all been older than her, with Thiodore's three sons Isaias, Thaddius, and Ferdinand already married some time ago. Isaias and Thaddius even had children of their own. Kristopher's two sons were closer to her age, but his younger one, Caius, had recently married. It was only Nolia and Kristopher's other son Cathrinus that still remained unwed.

Although she supposed that wouldn't be for long.

"I'll need to speak with my Uncle Kristopher regarding this betrothal," Nolia decided. "And I'd like to meet the next girl in line for the throne. I need to be certain they weren't members of Elias' coup."

"I'll arrange it immediately, Your Majesty," Thiodore said quickly.

Nolia nodded before taking a deep breath. "Speaking of betrothals, I think it's necessary to mention that I'm engaged."

There was a moment of silence before Rianne gasped. "To Mikael?" she exclaimed.

Nolia blanched, her lips parting, but not a sound coming from them.

Gristola all but glared at Rianne. "The boy that brought you to Alexie, who coincidentally is the brother of one of our council members?"

Nolia looked at Alexie, hoping that her panic wasn't obvious. When she'd become engaged to Isidore, she hadn't intended to tell anyone that he hadn't competed. But now Alexie's harmless explanation of events made it impossible.

"I'm engaged to a boy named Isidore," Nolia admitted. "He's the son of my mother's cousin, Isiris."

"Isiris?" Thiodore blurted out, sitting up straight. "She's *alive*?"

"And likely spying on us through that door," Alexie mumbled.

"Isiris disappeared years ago," Gristola commented with a frown. "Following the execution of her sister and nieces."

"How was her son allowed to compete?" Marvin asked. "Wouldn't he be too close in line for the throne?"

"He isn't, and he didn't compete," Nolia told them. She was unable to look any of them in the eye as she explained how she'd met and teamed up with Isiris, but their displeasure was palpable before she'd finished speaking.

"You can't marry a rebel!" Rianne cried out.

"Icarian queens *must* marry knights!" Marvin agreed.

"This boy and his mother deserve execution as much as the Girards do!" Gristola bellowed.

"No!" Nolia stood, slamming her palms against the table so hard it stung.

Everyone's attention quickly turned to the red-faced teenager who was tearing off the pearl diadem nestled in her hair.

"I'm the queen now, aren't I?" Nolia waved the headpiece at them. "And if I say that no one dies then they don't. And if I say that everyone dies then they *do*. Right now I'm telling you that I'm engaged to Isidore, and that he and his mother are going to be treated with the respect they deserve. Not only because they're my family, but because they helped save me." Her eyes narrowed, the fury almost making her shake. "Just like how I've already told you that Audrie and her family aren't going to be executed. They're going to be *protected*, and no, this isn't up for discussion. If anyone kills them, I will hunt them down and murder them with my bare hands for going against my word. Do you understand me?"

Thiodore was the first to move, kneeling so that he almost wasn't visible behind the table. "Yes, Your Majesty," he said.

Slowly the other council members followed his lead, kneeling as they agreed as well.

Nolia watched them, breathless. Her heart was still beating twice as fast, the rage burning through her veins. She was angry in a way that she'd never been before, especially after such little probing, all things considered. Was her new power already getting to her head? Corinne had always warned her that she was too conceited.

"I'm happy to hear that the matter is settled," Nolia said, keeping her tone level. "Is there anything else you wish to discuss?"

"Your coronation?" Rianne suggested quietly.

Nolia swallowed hard before nodding. "I'll find a planner."

7

Audrie

WHEN AUDRIE AWOKE, Nolia was gone, but she wasn't alone. Yadira was there, on Nolia's order, to keep her company. Neither girl seemed to be too happy about that.

They'd always been jealous of each other as long as Audrie could remember. Yadira, because Audrie was Nolia's best friend, and Audrie because Yadira was able to be with Nolia all of the time. Although now Audrie assumed she'd no longer have any reason to be jealous when she and Nolia could never be separated again. Perhaps now the person Audrie would be jealous of would be Isidore, even if the idea felt odd. She'd never thought it possible that a boy would come between her and Nolia.

Audrie was tempted to ask Yadira about how she dealt with sharing Nolia as the lady-in-waiting set down two plates of eggs, potatoes, and bacon along with two cups of chamomile tea in front of her.

"Is Nolia joining me?" Audrie asked, glancing around the tea room. Some of Nolia's ladies were sitting on the couches, reading or chatting. Some caught her eye, giving her mostly friendly smiles, but Audrie knew better than to trust them; most of them disliked her more than Yadira did for unintentionally putting them too far away from Nolia's favor. Audrie could see some noticing that she was still in the nightgown Nolia had let her borrow with messy hair from being slept on, and she pulled her robe around her tighter.

Yadira sat down, grabbing a golden fork as Audrie scooped potatoes into her mouth. "She's busy with her council."

Audrie tried not to look too disappointed as she chewed. "How has everything been since I last saw you?" she asked. *Since Corinne's funeral when we found out that Katrine was dead and Elias was trying to make himself king*, was what she really meant. Quite a bit had happened that day.

"I've been endlessly concerned," Yadira answered, stabbing an egg. "First for my princess and then for myself and her household. We had no idea what His Majesty intended to do with us since he was refusing to let us go home. We couldn't leave the crown princess's rooms."

Audrie grimaced. "But no one hurt you, right?"

"No one." Yadira's eyes landed on the guards hovering by the room's doorway. "We would have had some protection if they'd tried."

"That's good to hear." Audrie nibbled on a piece of bacon. "Nolia doesn't need any more loss in her life."

"She doesn't," Yadira agreed, hesitating to eat the potatoes on her fork. "I think that we should take her to Corinne's grave."

Audrie paused her eating too. She thought of the tears Nolia had spilt the night before and the guilt she carried. Guilt that Audrie understood, even if it was in a different way.

"You think it's a good idea?" Audrie asked.

Yadira nodded. "She was upset that we'd held a funeral without her. I was thinking of speaking with High Priestess Agnesia about arranging some sort of secondary blessing. I think it would make Her Majesty less sad to have missed the burial."

That's doubtful, Audrie thought, but her mouth was full, so she waited to respond. "Perhaps when more time has passed," she said. "I don't know if she'd be ready for that sort of thing. Especially seeing as how she has to learn how to run a queendom and put together an execution."

Yadira paled. "She can't ignore her pain in order to do those things. She has to feel them so she can do her new jobs well."

"After the execution," Audrie insisted. "Then she can mourn all of them at the same time."

Yadira crossed her arms. "All of them?" she repeated. "You think Nolia is going to need to mourn her father too? Do you even know her?"

"I know her better than you do," Audrie replied, waving her fork at her and making Yadira scowl. "But no, I don't think she'll want to mourn him, but she's *killing* someone. Maybe it's not by her own hand, and maybe she didn't love him very much, but it's something she's going to need time to come to terms with."

Audrie had tried to keep her tone light but knew she'd failed when Yadira's scowl was replaced with something that looked an awful lot like pity. Pity that Audrie wished she could feel for herself in the same way she did Nolia, but all she was filled with was guilt. The last thing she wanted was for Nolia to feel the same way, but there wasn't a way around it. Elias needed to die.

"Lady Yadira."

Audrie hadn't noticed a guard approaching them, and looked up suddenly at her, seeing one of the many guards that she didn't know but was hoping didn't work for Elias.

"Mikael and Cilia are requesting an audience with you."

"Of course, let them in." Yadira stood, brushing down her shimmery black skirts. She turned to one of the maids hovering by the door that apparently led to the kitchens and barked, "Get two more plates of breakfast."

Audrie raised her eyebrows at the entire exchange. "Since when are you friends with Mikael and his sister?" she asked.

"Since Princess Nolia introduced us."

"She's queen now," Audrie felt the need to remind her, and Yadira stuck her tongue out at her. "Also, don't you think I should change before—?"

But it was too late. The guard led in Mikael and a girl Audrie didn't recognize but assumed was his sister. Mikael looked as if he was about to bow to Yadira, but then he spotted her, seated at the table with a piece of bacon in her mouth. "Audrie," he blurted out instead.

Audrie smiled despite her embarrassment. Although she wasn't sure why her appearance mattered all that much when Mikael had seen her at her worst during the Competition. "Mikael, I'm so happy to see you," she said, wiping her mouth with a napkin before standing to greet him.

Mikael pulled her into a tight hug. "You're still a messy eater I see," he replied.

"Mikael," his sister scolded as Audrie laughed.

"Not as bad as when I was 'Levi' I hope," she said.

"Certainly not." Mikael let go of her, as if to examine her before realizing she was in a nightgown and his cheeks reddened. "Perhaps I should have sent word beforehand that I was coming."

"To be fair, you did say we were coming to see *Yadira*," Cilia pointed out.

Mikael turned to the lady-in-waiting, clearly having forgotten her existence. "Lady Yadira," he said with a bow. "Thank you for accepting our audience."

"Of course." Yadira clasped her hands in front of her, glancing between the siblings. "I was hoping to see you soon."

"I hope this was soon enough." Mikael motioned towards one of the windows at the early morning light.

"Certainly."

An awkward silence fell upon the group, and so Audrie decided to fill it, sticking her hand out to Mikael's sister. "We haven't been introduced," she said. "I'm Audrie, I'm—"

"The girl who pretended to be a boy and got my brother into a good deal of trouble," Cilia interrupted with a grin.

"That would be me," Audrie agreed.

"I'm Cilia," Cilia shook Audrie's hand. "Mikael's favorite sister, whether he's willing to admit it or not."

Mikael wrapped an arm around his sister's shoulders. "If I picked a favorite among you, the other seven would murder me," he reminded her. "I'd rather go on living."

Cilia shoved him away teasingly, and Audrie couldn't help but smile. It made her miss Levi despite having seen him the day before. It had been too brief, and she wondered if Nolia would be alright with freeing Levi to spend time with her while she was busy.

"I wasn't sure if you'd eaten or not," Yadira said as two maids appeared with plates for Mikael and Cilia. "Please join us."

"Thank you, that's very kind of you," Mikael said.

The group then sat, another awkward silence looming over them, before Cilia cleared her throat.

"I'm allergic to eggs," she announced.

Yadira's eyes widened in horror. "Oh, I'm so sorry, I—"

"It's no issue," Mikael quickly said, grabbing Cilia's plate to scrape the eggs onto his. "I can eat them. She can take some of my potatoes and bacon in exchange."

"Are you sure?" Yadira insisted, looking at Cilia who was seated in the chair to her right. "I can get you something else. Anything you want, all you have to say is—"

"This is fine." Cilia placed a calming hand over hers.

The two girls stared at each other for so long it became awkward again. But it was clear to Audrie that whatever understanding they needed to come to, they were too busy with that to pay attention to her or Mikael. So she used the chance to ask about the question she'd woken up with.

"I heard most of what happened to you two after I was kidnapped," Audrie told Mikael, being sure to keep her voice low in case Nolia's other ladies were being nosy—and they very likely were. "But we fell asleep before I could ask about Calix."

"Calix?" Mikael's eyes widened as if she'd struck him. "Nolia's guard? Why would you want to know anything about him? He's a guard, not anyone important."

Audrie rolled her eyes, and tried not to laugh. "Mikael, I'm her best friend," she said. "I *know*."

Mikael tilted his head. "You know?"

"Of course I know."

Mikael's panicked expression swiftly became a frown. "You shouldn't know," he said. "If they'd been caught, you would have been punished for not telling Their Majesties."

Audrie rolled her eyes again. "Nolia would have never told anyone that I knew, and Calix wasn't aware, and thank the gods for that. Now do you know what's happened to him or not?"

Mikael shook his head. "The last time I heard anything about him, we'd locked him in the washroom of Alexie's room."

Audrie glanced at Cilia and Yadira, who were now speaking quietly to each other. "Do you think that's all Nolia knows too?" she asked.

"Nolia would more likely tell you things than me," Mikael said with a shrug.

"Would she?" Audrie focused on him once more. "You've come a long way from being afraid to speak without her permission. Now you're referring to her by first name very casually."

Mikael blushed. "Only because she asked me to be so informal with her," he admitted.

Audrie's eyebrows shot up. Nolia had been raised with the knowledge of how important her title was, and to never allow anyone to disrespect her by forgetting it. She'd watched Nolia remind people to call her *Princess* or *Your Highness*, but she'd always insisted that Audrie call her by her first name. Now apparently she liked Mikael enough to do the same.

"I should have expected the two of you to grow close when I left you alone," Audrie mumbled.

"We're just friends," Mikael said quickly. "There isn't anything else happening between us."

"Of course there isn't." Audrie gave him a look. "She's engaged to someone else."

Mikael winced, picking up his fork again. "That she is."

• • •

They'd finished eating by the time that Nolia returned from the council meeting, and the now group of five settled into the tea room's couches, with Nolia and Audrie together on one, Mikael and Cilia on another, and Yadira alone.

"I wasn't expecting guests," Nolia said as she arranged her gown's pearl-studded ruffles around her.

"Neither was I," Audrie said, feeling all the more out of place next to Nolia's finery.

"Particularly," Nolia went on as if she hadn't spoken, her eyes trained on Mikael and Cilia, "the siblings of one of my council members."

Audrie's lips parted in surprise, and Cilia smacked Mikael's arm. "You never mentioned Rianne to Her Majesty?" she scolded.

Mikael smiled sheepishly. "I thought that she already knew."

"You never told me your surname," Nolia pointed out. "How was I supposed to know?"

Mikael's cheeks reddened, the thought clearly never having passed his mind as he apologized. "I promise I never meant to keep anything from you."

Nolia's gaze softened, and while she didn't say so, Audrie knew she'd already forgiven him.

"I would have told you if I'd realized that you weren't aware, Your Majesty," Cilia said. "I hope that this new information won't stop you from letting us take Yadira on a walk through the gardens."

Yadira immediately perked up.

"Us?" Mikael repeated.

"Yes, *us*." Cilia crossed her arms. "You need a chaperone."

Audrie bit back a laugh. "Why would you need...?" Her eyes widened as she glanced between Mikael and Yadira. "Wait, are you two supposed to be courting?!"

No one spoke, but their cringes were enough of a response to confirm she was right. At least it explained why everything had been awkward earlier, as well as why Yadira was trying so hard to please Cilia. She would certainly want Mikael's family's blessing.

"I can't say I expected this, but congratulations," Audrie stammered out.

Mikael and Yadira appeared uncomfortable, but not nearly as uneasy as Nolia was as she shifted on the couch. "I don't want to keep you two—or three—from your first outing together," she said.

"You're not—" Mikael began, but Nolia stopped him with her hand.

"It's alright." Nolia wore a tense smile. "The matter with your sister and your courtship. Please go."

Yadira, Mikael, and Cilia exchanged looks, but after a moment they obeyed, leaving the best friends alone in a heavy silence that stretched due to the distracted expression on Nolia's face.

"Did the council meeting go well?" Audrie asked.

"Yes and no." Nolia reached for her hand. "Apparently only a crowned monarch can arrange an execution, so I'll need to rush my coronation. Which is naturally difficult to do when I destroyed the crown I'm supposed to be crowned with. I'm having a new one made as quickly as possible."

Audrie nodded. "So until then Elias will remain alive?" she asked. "That's not too much of an issue so long as his remaining supporters don't try to rescue him." She sat up straighter, seeing her perfect opportunity to tell Nolia about Lia and Meriah, but Nolia continued before she could.

"That's not what I'm worried about," Nolia said. "I'm worried about *you* and your family. The council was very insistent that you should die because of your involvement in Elias' coup."

Audrie blanched. "They want to execute us?"

Nolia's grip around her fingers tightened. "I won't let them," she promised. "I lost my temper when they kept insisting. I think they finally understood, but I don't know if anyone else will. That's why it's imperative that your parents agree to tell me everything they know about Elias and his rebellion. Beginning with the people that they know supported him and likely still do."

Audrie's head was spinning, but she managed to blurt out, "I know others who can help too." She told her what had happened the day before with Lia and Meriah, and Darius.

"Gods, why didn't you tell me last night?" Nolia asked, exasperated. "Lia should go immediately to collect her sister and that Darius boy. I'm sure you don't want anything happening to him."

"I guess not," Audrie mumbled as her thoughts went to Rubin, Darius' boyfriend that he refused to name as such. She wondered if Nolia had freed Rubin and the other knights yet since they should have gone home long ago.

"You guess not?" Nolia snickered. "Audrie, you should see the way your eyes light up when you say his name."

Audrie's face warmed, and Nolia pulled her out of her seat before she could snipe back. They hooked their arms together, Nolia leading her towards the hallway as a guard trailed behind them.

"Where are we going?"

"To find you something from my closet to wear." Before Audrie could object, Nolia continued, "Then you'll tell Lia about my decision and round up your family."

A flurry of footsteps stopped Audrie from replying as she turned over her shoulder to see who was rushing towards them.

"Your Majesty."

It was the same guard that had announced Mikael and Cilia's arrival, this time accompanied by a maid.

"Yes, what is it?" Nolia stopped, turning Audrie along with her to face them.

"A letter has arrived for you."

Nolia raised an eyebrow but stuck her hand out. "A letter? Not a note?"

"Yes." The maid handed it to her before curtsying.

"Is there really a difference between the two?" Audrie asked as she crowded closer to Nolia to look at the thick piece of cream paper. *Nolia Riona, Queen of Icaria* had been scrawled on it in a hand she didn't recognize. The seal was an image of a dagger with wings, its end curved to make it look like a J.

Audrie froze, her heart beginning to race. "Nolia—"

Her best friend tore the letter open, angling it so Audrie could read it too.

Queen Nolia,
Firstly, I wish to give my condolences for the loss of Queen Katrine.
While she and I never were able to see eye to eye, I did admire her.
Secondly, I am sure you are aware of my many attempts in the past to
meet with your dearly departed mother. She was never interested in
working with me, and I hope that you instead will be inclined and
eager.
Thirdly, I understand that you have only just ascended and therefore
am willing to speak with an envoy of yours. If you so choose to accept
my assistance in making Icaria a better place for all who live here, I
will meet with your envoy at Dismund Palace in a day's time.
Justina

"Who gave this to you?" Nolia asked the maid. "Where's the messenger?"

"She left, Your Majesty," the maid answered. "That was why I was tasked with bringing it to you."

Nolia muttered a curse.

"This doesn't make any sense," Audrie mumbled. "Why would Just—?"

"I don't know," Nolia interrupted quickly, and Audrie realized that she likely didn't want her saying the rebel's name out loud. Before she could apologize, Nolia was nodding to the maid. "All I know is that I need you to bring me Isiris or Isidore. Now."

8

Nolia

DRESSES WERE THE best kind of distraction. Nolia had so many that she could spend hours trying them on if she wanted, and that was before she'd inherited Katrine's wardrobe. The queen had more gowns than Nolia would ever know what to do with.

Nolia had avoided staring at them the night before and that morning when getting dressed, but now she'd complicated matters. All because she'd insisted that Audrie pick whatever she wanted from the queen's closet.

"This one's beautiful," Audrie gushed, pulling one of the gowns off the hook to get a better look. "Don't you think?"

"It's lovely," Nolia agreed, her eyes on the cupboard of headpieces. If she had to wear something that belonged to her mother, it would be those since there was no option. Crowns were meant to be passed down from queen to queen.

"I think I love this one more."

Nolia spotted a tiara glittering with emeralds that she didn't think she'd ever seen Katrine put on, and for good reason. It reminded her of her father's eyes. "You should wear it."

"No, I actually like this one more."

"You can have it." Nolia picked up a gold diadem of rubies, and she made a mental note to wear it with Katrine's ring once it was returned to her. She frowned then, wondering what had become of the queen's jewelry collection.

"Actually, do you think this color would look good on me?"

"It'll look gorgeous on you," Nolia replied, glancing at the vanity. Had Katrine organized her jewelry inside of its multitude of drawers? She didn't know why it wouldn't be on display along with everything else.

"Nolia."

"Hm?" Nolia stepped over to the vanity, opening the first drawer which only revealed a variety of brushes.

"You haven't looked at anything I've picked out."

Nolia opened another drawer, this one filled with pins and ribbons. "I don't have to look to know you'll look beautiful in whatever you pick."

"*Nolia.*"

"What?" The teenage queen sighed before catching her best friend's eye in the reflection of the vanity mirror.

"If you don't want to look at your mother's dresses with me, you don't have to," Audrie said. "You don't have to let me wear any of them either."

Nolia swallowed. "Nonsense," she said. "You need something to wear. You can't conduct official royal business in a nightgown, and I can't believe Yadira didn't put you in anything before serving you breakfast. Tomorrow I'll be certain she does."

"Tomorrow?" Audrie repeated. "We've never had sleepovers back-to-back."

Because Corinne would have never let us, Nolia thought as she straightened, her search for the queen's jewelry momentarily forgotten. She'd always been so worried about propriety that it ruined their fun half the time.

"You don't have to," she said. "If you'd rather sleep in your own bed, I understand."

"My 'own bed' is at Dismund," Audrie said. "And I'm not going back there, at least not anytime soon. But that's not what this is about."

"What *is* this about?"

Audrie hesitated, turning to grab another gown. "I don't want to get used to this," she told her. "You're engaged, and you won't be forever. Eventually you'll have a husband who won't appreciate someone else sleeping next to his wife."

Nolia scoffed. "You're my best friend, not my lover."

"I don't think he'll like it." Audrie reached for another gown. "At least not half as much as I like this dress."

Nolia averted her gaze.

"I knew you were uncomfortable," Audrie said accusingly.

"Audrie, I—"

"Go," Audrie told her. "Wait outside while I pick something that I can put on by myself."

Nolia relaxed, and she almost laughed. "Are you banishing me from my own closet?"

"I certainly am," Audrie replied. "Get out!"

Nolia rolled her eyes, but was glad for the opportunity to escape. She returned to the queen's bedroom where she snatched Justina's letter from the mantle where she'd left it next to Katrine's family portrait.

Before Nolia could reread it again, Giana knocked and poked her head inside of the bedroom. "Queen Nolia, it's—"

"Let her in."

"But it's not—"

"Let him in." Nolia waved wildly at the guard.

"Into your *bedroom*?" Giana's eyes widened as if it was the most scandalous idea in the world.

Nolia hesitated a moment before reaffirming. Allowing Isidore into her room before they were married wasn't ideal, but it wasn't as if they would be alone. Audrie was there, and Isiris would be too once someone found her. That would be two witnesses to confirm that nothing improper had occurred.

The golden door widened, and Giana stepped in first, a boy that looked nothing like Isidore behind her.

"Mikael?" Nolia blurted out in surprise.

"Your Majesty." He bowed, his eyes quickly scanning her. "Your guards were in a panic, and I was afraid something had happened to you."

Nolia almost glared at Giana, who shrugged with a look that said, *I tried to tell you.* "When Isiris or Isidore arrive, send them in," she told the guard. "Anyone else can remain outside."

Giana nodded, pointedly leaving the door to the queen's bedroom half open.

"Did you come alone?" Nolia asked as Giana went past the sitting room and through the entrance of the queen's apartment.

"Alone? Yes, why wouldn't I...?" Mikael's eyes widened and he blushed. "I'm afraid I left Yadira with my sister in the gardens after your guards questioned us."

Nolia had to bite back a smile, hating how endearing she found his embarrassment. Especially since it was because he'd abandoned her friend, the girl he was *courting*.

"Is that Mikael?" Audrie's voice rang out from the closet.

"Yes," Nolia called back.

"Audrie's here?" Mikael glanced in the direction of her voice.

"She's changing," Nolia explained. "She couldn't wear my nightgown all day."

"Wow." Mikael's lips twisted into a small smile. "My sisters despise sharing clothing, and you're a queen who has no issue letting your best friend borrow yours."

Nolia shrugged, avoiding his eyes. "Perhaps it's because I *don't* have sisters that I'm so willing to share. I also did like how upset Corinne would get whenever she saw Audrie in one of my gowns. She found it improper for me to let someone else wear my clothing, although the dresses Audrie picks are never ones I wear. We have two very different styles..."

She knew she was rambling now, but Mikael didn't seem to care as he laughed. "Nonetheless, I think you're a very generous person, Nolia."

Nolia's heart skipped a beat at the use of her first name coming from Mikael's mouth. "You're just being kind," she mumbled. "I'm actually rather selfish and vain and—"

"You're too hard on yourself," Mikael said, and when Nolia looked up at him, she nearly melted under the softness of his gaze.

"Perhaps you should go," Nolia forced herself to say. "Now that you know I'm alright."

"Do you not want my help?" Mikael asked. "With whatever it is that you need Isiris and Isidore for?"

Nolia hesitated, staring at the letter in her hands as she considered whether or not Mikael could do anything. She wasn't certain he knew all that much more about the rebel than she did, and there was no way he knew anything about how involved she'd been with Elias. But was there something else she was missing?

"I know it isn't the two of us anymore," Mikael said quietly. "I know that you have a team of people now who will do whatever you ask of them. I know that there's others you may trust more than you do me. But perhaps you can allow me to continue helping you?"

Nolia gazed at him, remembering the dream Mikael had described to her about them. How he was supposed to compete, not because he was meant to be king, but because he and Nolia would need each other.

"I do want your help," Nolia admitted. "But I don't want you to feel obligated to offer it."

"I don't," Mikael answered firmly. "I'm here because I want to be with you." His face reddened, as if realizing how it sounded. "Not *with* you, here for you, I didn't mean—"

But Nolia stopped listening. Her heart was already beating so loudly in her ears, she couldn't have heard him if she wanted to. She watched his lips moving, and the way his jade green eyes flashed as he looked at her. She wondered what it would be like to touch his face, to run her fingers over his smooth skin.

"Your Majesty?"

Nolia blinked, knowing that the voice hadn't come from Mikael since she was still staring at his lips.

"Queen Nolia?"

She turned to her door, slowly being crept all the way open.

"Isidore," Nolia blurted out, nearly jumping away from Mikael despite the distance between them. "Come in, is your mother —?"

"I'm right here." Isiris strode past her son into the room. "To think I grew up visiting Candicia often and have never been allowed in here before."

"Neither was I until last night."

Nolia hadn't realized she'd spoken the thought out loud until everyone was staring at her.

"Monarchs are cold people," Isiris commented, returning to examining the room until she spotted the fireplace mantle. She focused on the small portrait before looking at Nolia again. "Although that doesn't mean *you* have to be. It's difficult not to repeat your parents' mistakes, but not impossible so long as you try."

A heavy silence filled the room, and Nolia grasped the letter tighter as she tried to find words. She was saved by the appearance of Audrie, bounding out of her closet in a deep red gown made of a shimmering satin cloth with bell sleeves.

"Wow," Mikael blurted out, and Nolia was unable to stop herself from glaring at him. He didn't notice as he added, "Sometimes I still forget you're a girl."

This time Audrie glared at him, and Isidore stifled a laugh.

"I hope you didn't summon us here for a fashion show," Isiris said dryly.

"No." Nolia glanced at Mikael. "Would you escort Audrie to her parents' room before returning to Cilia and Yadira?" When disappointment flashed across his face, she added, "I'll need you for something else soon enough."

"I can't imagine why you would need him for anything," Isiris commented as he and Audrie left. "Especially when you have such a strong, handsome—"

Nolia placed the letter in Isidore's hands, ignoring his red face like she was ignoring her own. "I need your help," she said. "I have no idea how much you know about the other rebels working with Elias, but I figured you were my best chance of knowing the truth."

"Justina?" Isiris raised her eyebrows as she read the letter over Isidore's shoulder.

Nolia nodded, clasping her empty hands in front of her. "Justina."

• • •

Elias had given Cecily and Josip a rather nice room. The front doors opened into a sitting room with three red couches arranged in a half circle around an unlit marble fireplace. In the middle of them was a large black carpet that matched nicely with the curtains that hung on both sides of the fireplace and the four walls' black paneling.

Cecily and Josip had seemingly been in the middle of tea at the round table, made from a reddish wood, that had been placed behind the couch that faced the fireplace.

Upon further inspection, Nolia realized that only one cup in the set had been used. She didn't know why that interested her, only that it did.

"Stand, I'd like to sit and chat with you," Nolia told the Girards as she stepped around their kneeling forms to get to one of the couches.

"Have we done something else wrong?" Josip asked, ignoring Cecily who clearly needed assistance standing back up. "Have we birthed your father another bastard?"

"Hey," Levi objected as he helped his mother.

"If you've done anything else worthy of punishment, I haven't discovered it," Nolia replied as she spread her skirts out around her before she sat. Audrie nestled next to her. "I'm here because I have more questions."

"What more do you need to know?" Josip grouched, sitting alone on the couch next to where Levi and Cecily had settled.

Nolia frowned at him. "Something to convince my council that your family shouldn't be executed."

"Your council wants to kill us?" Levi asked, his eyes widening.

"Unfortunately," Nolia said. "It won't happen without my word, but I'd like to prove that I'm making the correct decision. Which leads me to you." Nolia's eyes returned to Josip. "How closely did you know the rebels you worked with?"

Josip leaned back into the couch, his eyes lighting with understanding. "You're going to hunt them down, aren't you?" he asked. "You have Isiris on your side and now you want all of them?"

No, Nolia wanted to say, but she did want to eliminate any support for Elias. She didn't believe any other rebel groups would commit themselves as loyally as Isiris had, so she didn't want them to work for her. She simply wanted them to disband and not cause her the trouble they had Katrine.

"We're curious about a specific rebel, Father," Audrie said. "Justina."

"Justina?" Josip froze. "What about her?"

"Was she one of Elias' rebels?"

"No," Josip said, shaking his head so hard it looked painful. "We tried multiple times to recruit her, but she always refused. She... she even threatened us to leave her be." The words hung in the air for a moment before he added, "She's nothing but trouble. No one knows what she really wants since it certainly isn't money. She may simply want to destroy Icaria. I think we're lucky she never agreed to work for His Majesty."

Nolia carefully considered his words and the genuine fear on Josip's face. Whatever his experience had been with Justina, it hadn't been a positive one. She was more unsure of what to do now. Isiris and Isidore hadn't been able to tell her who most of the other rebels that Elias had hired were. They'd only ever worked with two other groups, who Isiris was already planning to capture soon. All Nolia had truly learned from that conversation was that Isiris hated Justina and strongly advised against meeting with her.

"Thank you for enlightening us on the matter," Nolia answered, standing along with Audrie. "I'd like the information of the other rebel groups you've worked with as well."

Josip hesitated before nodding. "As you wish."

"Your Majesty." Cecily stood to offer a weak curtsy. "If it's Justina you're curious about, perhaps you should speak to your father." Josip shot her a dirty look, but Cecily ignored him. "I know he reached out to her again recently, this time personally. He was very secretive about it, and since he never shared anything with me, I didn't think anything about it. I suppose he didn't share the result of the attempt with Josip either."

"Of course he did," Josip answered. "She's *always* denied him."

"How do you know if she did this time?" Cecily asked. "I've been with you every single time you've spoken to Elias this past week, and he didn't mention anything about it. It's possible she declined or never responded. But it's also possible she changed her mind after seeing him take the throne."

A terrible idea came to mind, and Nolia offered Audrie her arm before nodding to Cecily. "Thank you," she said. "I'll see what I can do about that matter."

Then before they could notice her trembling, Nolia strode out of the room with Audrie.

"Should Levi—?"

"He can stay with your parents for now. It's not as if he's going to plan anything sinister with them."

Giana shut the doors to Audrie's parents' room behind them, and when Nolia turned to look at her guard, she spotted a flash of red barreling towards her.

"You cursed crown! You sit on a throne of innocent blood!"

The guards sprang into action, two knocking the woman over and the others surrounding Nolia and Audrie, their swords unsheathed as they ushered the girls away.

"You monster, you coward!" the woman continued to shriek. "My family died in your honor, and yet you refuse them a proper burial?"

Nolia stopped, and Giana bumped into her back.

"Your Majesty—?"

"What's she talking about?" Nolia interrupted, keeping her voice low.

"I think she means what Elias did," Audrie answered when Giana hesitated. "He didn't exactly say it, but I'm fairly certain he killed all of the nobles who wouldn't support him."

Nolia barely stifled a gasp, unsure of why she found the news so surprising. It sounded exactly like something Elias would do.

"Let me speak to her," Nolia told her guards. "And have someone find all of the nobles Elias killed immediately."

9

Audrie

AUDRIE THOUGHT THAT Nolia's meeting with her parents was awkward, but it wasn't anything compared to this one. Nolia wouldn't sit on the queen's throne, hovering instead on the platform where the king's and crown princess's thrones sat, while the woman who'd tried to attack her was refusing to kneel, struggling with the guards forcing her down.

"Well," Nolia said, sounding irritated. "I'm so happy to see that you're cooperating after I so kindly made time for you, Miss ...?"

The woman's brown eyes glinted in the light. "Don't you recognize me?"

Nolia frowned. "I don't, I'm sorry."

The woman let out a sound that was half laugh and half sigh. "I'm Beatrix," she said.

Nolia's frown deepened before the memory seemingly clicked. Her nostrils flared as she glared at the woman. "You're no noble," she said. "You're my father's latest plaything."

Audrie was proud of herself for not gasping as she looked at the woman with new eyes. She was rather pretty, despite her current state of disarray, and was older than she would have thought Elias would be interested in. Audrie wondered whether or not her mother had known about Beatrix. She'd only married Elias to legitimize Alaric, but Audrie had seen Elias flirt with her recently, and Cecily had been flattered. If they'd truly been married, would Cecily have allowed him to continue having mistresses? Audrie didn't think she would.

"I believed myself to be his only," Beatrix admitted. "At least until he married his bastard's mother."

"I'm certain there are more of you," Nolia replied, rolling her eyes.

Beatrix shrugged. "Not quite like me."

"Perhaps not," Nolia agreed after a moment. "Any other mistress of Elias likely wouldn't have family members killed by his hand. Assuming you were telling the truth about that?"

Beatrix's face fell. "I wasn't lying," she said quietly. "My family wouldn't support him, and no matter how much I begged them... no matter how much I pleaded with him to forgive them for my sake..."

Audrie crossed her arms. So Elias had been in contact with his mistress during the days he was planning his wedding to someone else. She would have to tell Cecily about this whenever she got the chance.

Nolia sighed. "Don't worry about your family. Once we find wherever your lover hid their bodies, they'll be given to you for a proper burial."

"Thank you," Beatrix sniffled.

"Don't assume you're safe." Nolia's gaze hardened again. "You clearly had the intention of attacking me earlier, and I have no idea how you were able to wander the hallways in the first place. Not to mention, your lack of decorum the last time we met."

Beatrix paled.

"I did tell you I would remember it when I became queen."

Audrie waited eagerly for either woman to elaborate, and she could tell the guards were curious too as they stared between the queen and mistress.

"Will you kill me along with my family?" Beatrix asked.

Nolia pretended to consider her question, and Audrie had to bite back a smile. *Of course* Nolia wouldn't kill her, and it was stupid of the woman to think she would.

"Have you done anything treasonous?"

"I've only done two things wrong in my life," Beatrix answered. "I ruined my chances of a suitable marriage by sleeping with a married man and shamed my family. Then I became pregnant with his child."

Nolia blanched, and this time Audrie wasn't able to stop herself from gasping.

"You liar," Nolia hissed, looking ready to fly down the steps to strangle her. "My father has slept with over a hundred women since coming to Candicia, and only two have ever fallen pregnant."

Beatrix shrugged again. "I'm now the third."

"Lies," Nolia repeated, shaking her head. "If you actually are pregnant, it isn't by him."

"He's my child's father," Beatrix insisted. "What reason do I have to lie? What reason do I have to make you dislike me *more*? What reason do I have to make you desire to kill me when I've only just avoided dying?"

Nolia's eyes trailed down to Beatrix's stomach, and she appeared to be biting back other words as she asked, "Did you tell him you were pregnant?"

"Yes." Beatrix swallowed. "I found out during the Competition, but after you escaped, he brought Cecily to the palace and... I wasn't able to say anything until I was begging him to spare my family. He thought I was trying to manipulate him."

Like you're trying to manipulate us? Audrie thought, and she knew Nolia was thinking the same.

The queen stared so long at the mistress that Audrie wondered if she thought Beatrix would take her words back if she were intimidated enough.

"My previous promise stands," Nolia finally said. "You'll be given your family's bodies for burial. In the meantime, you'll be taken to the infirmary and later locked away. Whether that be in a cell or a very comfortable room all depends on your honesty."

Nolia flicked her hand, and the guards pulled Beatrix out of the room. This time she didn't fight them, but she didn't help them either, making them lift her up as her feet dragged on the marble floor.

It left a sour taste in Audrie's mouth, even after the throne room doors slammed shut.

Nolia stepped down from the platform and reached her arm out for Audrie to tangle hers through. "Let's go," she said.

"Where?" Audrie asked.

Nolia gave her a miserable smile. "I need you to do me a favor."

•••

It was an excellent plan. Audrie hadn't thought that it wouldn't be since after years of being taught by Icaria's—and some of the mainland's—most intelligent people, Nolia had no choice but to be incredibly smart. She just didn't understand why Isiris needed to be involved.

"I won't be able to speak once we step inside," Nolia was telling them. "And he can't be able to see me, but I'll stay close enough to be able to listen in. If that turns out to be somehow within your view, don't under any circumstances stare at me. I don't want him to catch on."

"I understand, Your Majesty," Isiris said. "You don't have to worry about *me*. I'll do everything perfectly."

"So will I," Audrie snapped.

"You both will," Nolia said, giving them a confident smile. "Now everyone be quiet."

They approached the doors of a place that Audrie had prayed she'd never have to return to, and she *never* prayed. The gods never seemed to hear her, and this was yet another piece of evidence proving they didn't care to listen or simply didn't exist. But Nolia—and her mother—would kill her if she claimed the latter.

"Your Majesty."

The guards bowed, and Nolia nodded in greeting. "I'd like for you to lead us to Elias."

A rush of pain stung Audrie's body as she stepped into the dark and dirty dungeon. She would have collapsed from the shock of it if her mind hadn't been conscious enough to tell her it was only phantom pain. It was nothing but a memory of how she'd felt when she'd first entered the dungeon. The sword wound she'd suffered in the second trial of the Competition had been infected and she'd had a concussion at the time, both without her knowing.

Nolia squeezed her arm, her royal blue eyes bright enough in the dark for Audrie to see her concern. *Are you alright?* they were asking.

Audrie only nodded. Now wasn't the time to relive the trauma of her short stay there. Nolia needed her.

They followed the guard silently through the many different hallways of the dungeon, winding around as if it were a maze. The space had purposely been built to be confusing so as to stop any prisoners from escaping if they somehow did get out of their cells.

"He's up ahead," the guard announced, and the group stopped. "Right in this next hallway."

"Excellent," Isiris said, not bothering to keep her voice down. "You may leave us."

Nolia nodded her agreement, and so the guard left, glancing back at them in case they weren't certain.

Audrie couldn't help but frown. Why was he so worried about them talking to Elias? Especially when Isiris had pointed out the obvious: he couldn't harm them. Or could he?

Nolia let go of Audrie, her confident smile doing nothing to soothe her newfound concerns as she motioned for her and Isiris to move. Isiris eagerly obeyed, and Audrie trailed after her, trying desperately to clear her mind.

"Elias." Isiris hadn't rounded the corner yet, but she called his name out loudly. "The king who failed to be a king."

Elias had been placed in the middle cell of a set of three. It was the largest one, but the cot inside still appeared cramped up against the wall. Audrie almost wanted to complain that she hadn't been given one, and her cell certainly could have fit it without an issue. It made her curious as to why this cell in particular had been chosen for the old king.

"Isiris." Elias didn't stand, but he did fix his slouch, causing his large bare stomach to stick out. Evidently, no one had thought to give him a shirt after wrapping his chest in bandages. "My closest ally," he said as he pressed a hand to the spot where she'd shot him.

Isiris laughed humorlessly. "If I was your closest ally, you certainly didn't have any friends."

"Yes," Elias answered, "I suppose that's the issue with purchasing the loyalty of people like you. Once someone comes along and offers a higher price, you're gone."

"Your little rebellion will fall apart in no time," Isiris agreed. "Particularly since you'll have lost a supporter as influential as Justina."

"Justina?" Elias repeated, raising his eyebrows. "Is that why you're here?" He laughed, although it sounded more like a wheeze as he grabbed his chest again. "You know damn well that she never agreed to side with me. She was too desperate to work with Katrine."

Audrie looked at Isiris, who didn't meet her gaze. They should have known that Elias would deny anything they asked about. But Nolia was counting on them not to let him get away with it.

"You don't have to lie," Audrie finally spoke up. "Especially not to me."

Elias' eyes shot to her, and she'd been prepared to receive his icy gaze. Instead, his emerald eyes softened.

"You look so much like him."

He'd commented on her resemblance to Alaric before, back when he'd thought she was Levi at the Competition. She wondered now if she could somehow use that to her advantage.

"My mother has shared a lot of things with me since yesterday," Audrie said. "One of them was that you were speaking with

Justina. Why would you do that if you didn't have a desire to work with her?"

Elias scowled. "Marrying your mother was a mistake," he spat out. "I should have known she wouldn't hesitate to betray me either."

"That's rather ironic considering you betrayed your wife for her," Isiris muttered.

"You're one to talk. You attempted to *kill* me!"

"That's different; I'm not your wife," Isiris said. "Besides, if I'd genuinely wanted to kill you, you'd be dead."

"You expect me to believe you nicked my heart on purpose?" Elias answered.

"You're aware of my skills with a bow."

"No woman is that skilled in archery or combat of any kind."

"What about diplomacy?" Isiris asked, grinning like she relished in lying to him. "I did bring you your daughter, didn't I?"

Elias stopped, staring at Audrie again as if debating how to respond.

"Cecily told me I'm your daughter." Audrie forced herself to step close enough to the cell that he could touch her if he wanted. "She says she lied to protect you. She thought Katrine wouldn't be able to stand another embarrassment like that and would annul your marriage."

When Elias remained silent, Audrie continued to push. "Nolia wants to kill you, but you know how much she loves me. If I tell her that I don't want her to kill my father, especially because we've been kept from each other, she won't. She'll let us get to know each other. Do you want that?"

Elias' face slowly twisted into a smile. "Audrie, my beautiful girl," he said, and she relaxed. She'd been convincing enough to make him believe she was his daughter, but had she been convincing enough for him to tell her about Justina? And the other rebels? And—?

Elias spat on her feet.

Audrie jumped away, shrieking as she felt the bottom of her borrowed gown brush against her ankles. How had he spit so far?

"You're not my child," Elias said. "Even if you want to believe that your mother lied, I've had no role in your life. I wasn't convinced enough to claim you when you were born, and I certainly won't now. Your love for Nolia is stronger than it ever would be for me, and what good are two daughters who want me dead?"

Audrie's hands curled into fists and her cheeks warmed. "I'm glad you didn't raise me," she snapped. "I'd be as selfish and horrible and—"

"Don't forget that I raised your best friend," Elias interrupted. "Any terrible thing you have to say about me, you'll only be saying about her too."

Audrie rolled her eyes. "*Corinne* raised her."

"And I hired Corinne." Elias' eyes shone with spite. "A governess from Espin, where I was born and raised. She was the perfect person to raise Nolia to be like me."

Audrie's heart began to beat wildly. "Nolia's nothing like you," she told him.

"Isn't she?"

Audrie was reminded of the exact same sentiment that Meriah and Lia had expressed the day before. Was Nolia truly so similar to her father?

"Why don't you make this conversation worth our time?"

Elias' eyes were still on Audrie as he told Isiris, "Justina is as uninterested in working with me as I am with her."

Another lie, Audrie thought, but at least this one could be proven.

"Then I believe you can tell us where you buried the bodies of the nobles you murdered," Isiris said. "The mother of your latest child is incredibly upset regarding the matter."

Elias turned to her sharply. "What are you talking about?"

Isiris smirked. "Where are the bodies?"

Elias glared at her before crossing his arms. "What will I receive in exchange for telling you?"

"You can keep your life," Isiris replied, her fingers settling over the sword sheathed at her side. Audrie wished that she'd thought to bring a weapon too.

Elias rolled his eyes. "Don't pretend that you came here with permission to kill me," he said. "Give me a true trade and I'll tell you."

"Fine," Isiris said. "I'll have someone bring you one of your favorite bottles of wine."

"And a proper meal," Elias said. "Preferably roasted pig."

Isiris scoffed. "You can have your wine or nothing at all."

"You can have an answer or nothing at all," Elias responded, his lip curling into a snarl.

"I'd rather we have nothing at all." Isiris spun around and strode away.

Wait! Audrie wanted to call after her. Nolia had trusted them to get this one piece of information for her. How could they leave without it?

"You'll get me what I want, won't you?"

Audrie slowly turned towards Elias, whose eyes were now on her. "A proper meal and drink for your father?"

Audrie swallowed. "I thought you said you weren't my father."

Elias continued to stare, and Audrie knew it wasn't her he was seeing; it was his son, her brother, that she'd murdered. "I can pretend," Elias said softly.

So can I—for Nolia, Audrie thought after a moment's hesitation. She nodded. "Where are the bodies?" she asked.

Elias smiled as if he'd won something despite the bars he was imprisoned behind. "Shouldn't it be obvious?" he said. "I had them taken to the Tower of Icaria."

• • •

"Thank the gods *one* of you has enough patience for my father."

Nolia's arm was threaded through Audrie's as she glared past her towards Isiris.

"Your Majesty doesn't have the patience for him," Isiris replied. "What makes you think that the rest of us should?"

Nolia rolled her eyes, clearly not wanting to argue the matter, and Audrie was glad. Nolia had been doing nothing but thanking her when she didn't quite feel like she was deserving of it. Not when there was so much dread filling her stomach.

No one likes to look at dead bodies, Audrie told herself. It was part of why they were keeping their distance from the tower, waiting for the group of guards that Nolia had asked to investigate to get inside. It'd taken some time for someone to find one of the few keys to the tower, as well as wind through the charred remains of the maze, but they'd have their answer soon enough. Audrie could close her eyes when they extracted the bodies, or better yet, she could leave the area altogether. She wouldn't have to see anything if she didn't want to.

Yet, Audrie's dread wouldn't disappear.

"Thank you again for getting the answer out of him," Nolia murmured to Audrie, smiling as she patted her arm. "I don't know what I would do without you."

Some of the dread lessened, and Audrie was almost able to smile back. At least until she heard the boom of an explosion.

Audrie and Nolia screamed, their voices intermingling with that of many others. Others who Audrie knew were close enough to the explosion to have been harmed.

"Run!" Isiris shouted at them.

Nolia was paralyzed in fear, looking terrifyingly similar to the way she had when Corinne had been shot.

"Audrie." Isiris' wild gaze found Audrie's. "Take her *now!*"

Audrie didn't need to be asked twice. She let go of Nolia's arm, grasping her hand instead to drag her along behind her.

Screams and cries of pain echoed behind them, and Audrie saw a flurry of movement before them as people streamed out of Candicia to see what had happened.

"Audrie," Nolia croaked.

"We're alright," Audrie tried to comfort her as Nolia pulled on her hand. "We're at a safe distance now, we're—"

The crack of stone interrupted her, and Audrie was no longer able to fight Nolia's insistence. She stopped in her tracks, and the best friends turned to watch as the once indestructible Tower of Icaria fell apart into chunks of rubble.

"What in the gods' names?" Audrie whispered.

"This wasn't the gods." Nolia's grip was weak in her hand. "This was him, this was my father. Trying to destroy Icaria starting with our most important tradition: the Competition."

10

Nolia

NOLIA DIDN'T SLEEP that night. She couldn't have if she'd wanted to. Her mind was stuck on the tower, watching it fall apart over and over again.

The daughter she prayed she'd have one day would never step inside of it to await the knight the gods supposedly wanted her to marry. The Icarian people wouldn't send their sons off to try to win her hand in marriage. There could be no Competition of Knights without the Tower of Icaria.

Nolia felt guilty for wondering if her father's allies had done her some sort of good in knocking the tower down. After all, she'd never wanted to participate in the Competition. She'd never wanted to marry a boy Elias would be picking out for her. She'd never wanted to marry someone she would hate as much as Katrine did Elias.

Nolia found that she hated him possibly as much as her mother did when she rose in the morning to news from the guards securing the area around the tower. He hadn't lied about the nobles' bodies being inside, not that there was very much left of them after the explosion. How he'd planned for the bombs to be planted inside since his imprisonment, Nolia wasn't certain, but she was going to find out.

Nolia gathered Audrie, Levi, Isiris, Isidore, Mikael, Cilia, and her council—save for Thiodore, who unlike the other members had returned home after their last meeting—in the throne room. Alexie, Isiris, and Mikael appeared to be the most awake among the group, and Nolia felt bad for having woken them. But they were who she trusted most to help her.

"Thank you for coming." Nolia smoothed down the cascading ruffles on the front of the skirt of the cream gown she'd changed into that morning. She'd also bathed and had Yadira put her newly washed hair into a high ponytail. A white gold sapphire tiara had been added and it peeked out, shining between her curls.

"It's not as if we had a choice."

All eyes turned to Levi, who blinked sleepily.

"Did I say that out loud?" he asked, and Audrie shoved him.

"Regardless of your choice in being here," Nolia said, "I'm going to give you a choice in whether or not you do what I'm asking of you. Which is to interrogate the palace staff regarding their loyalties."

The group glanced at each other, as if daring one of them to decline.

When they didn't, Nolia smiled. "I'll take your silence as agreement?" Her body relaxed even though her mind had told her over and over that she wouldn't have anything to worry about. It made her wonder if the less trusting part of her would always believe no one would ever desire to help her succeed as queen.

"If you're going to interrogate the palace guards, I can vouch for my own army," Alexie said. "None of them wanted Elias on the throne, and they were more than willing to fight for the correct heir to be placed upon it."

Nolia nodded. "Your guards can interrogate the others."

"I can vouch for my people as well," Isiris spoke up, crossing her arms. "They trust me, and so long as I remain loyal to you, they will be too."

"I'm sure Her Majesty wants people who are loyal to the crown," Isidore said.

"They're loyal to you too, and you're about to become king," Isiris replied. "They won't be an issue." She glanced at Nolia. "Although if she's concerned about strengthening loyalties, perhaps it's time to begin planning the wedding."

"In due time," Nolia snapped, her cheeks warming as she turned towards Levi and Cilia. "Are you comfortable speaking with the servants?"

They both nodded, and Audrie leaned over to Levi, whispering loudly, "Don't go falling in love with any more maids, especially if they're spies." Then he was the one to shove her, and while Nolia was curious to hear about who this crush of his was, she set her gaze on her council.

"I'd like for you to talk to the nobles who decided to support Elias," Nolia told them. "Many of you already have relationships with them, so I'm hoping it'll make them more willing to be honest."

When her council nodded, Nolia turned to Audrie and Mikael. "Since you'd know them best, I want you to interrogate the knights."

"The knights?" Audrie repeated with a frown. "I wouldn't say I know any of them, except for my roommates."

"And Rubin," Mikael added.

Nolia shrugged. "Someone needs to talk to them before they leave."

"Then that's what we'll do," Mikael answered. "Right, Audrie?"

"Right," Audrie agreed, her smile soothing Nolia.

"Good," Nolia said. "Alexie's soldiers that aren't interrogating other guards can help the rest of you round up the nobles, servants, and knights." Before Isiris could open her mouth, she quickly added, "And once Isidore has deemed a rebel loyal enough, they can interrogate guards. Are we in agreement?"

"Yes, Your Majesty," the group chorused, some much more seriously than others, and Nolia would have smiled at their teasing if she weren't so stressed about the things she had to do. Candicia was in a lockdown after the fall of the tower, with no one allowed to come or leave without Nolia's specific permission, but that couldn't last forever. Eventually the nobles' families would come looking, much like Beatrix had.

Beatrix. She was another issue entirely that Nolia had no time for at the moment. Her father's former mistress would have to stay secluded and out of the way until she decided what to do with her and her child. A child that Nolia still wasn't certain she believed was Elias' or that Beatrix was carrying, despite the physician's confirmation.

One problem at a time, Nolia tried to tell herself as she dismissed the group. First, she would check on the extraction of the bodies from the tower before—

"Your Majesty, your uncle and his family have arrived."

Nolia blinked at the guard in front of her. She'd been so lost in her own thoughts, she hadn't noticed they'd left the throne room or that the guard had appeared in front of her.

"Kristopher?" Nolia asked. She hadn't been expecting him until the afternoon, and she'd planned for a grand late lunch. Her cooks wouldn't be happy about this change.

Nolia nodded to the guard. "Let my uncle know I'll be with him shortly."

• • •

The royal dining room was reserved for important guests, usually mainland ambassadors, since they were the closest thing Icaria would ever get to hosting an actual monarch. The space was also used on holidays when Katrine invited her favorite nobles to dine with her. Nolia had never been included.

Elias hadn't either. The parties he hosted were in the bronze room which he used as both a dining room and dance floor since it was large enough. He had last used it for the knights during the Competition.

It wasn't anything near as elegant as the room Nolia entered. The white walls had gold panels and multiple portraits of different sizes. She spotted beautiful illustrations of the five Icarian palaces among them as well as one of Katrine on her throne, in a violet gown and the crown of Icaria on her head. There was a large crystal chandelier and the light from the floor-to-ceiling windows reflected off the gems, lighting up the walls in small rainbows.

"Your Majesty."

Five people stood to greet her, but only one approached her.

"Uncle Kristopher," Nolia said, almost marveling how it could be that he was younger than Thiodore but looked older. His black hair had almost completely grayed and his large brown eyes were deep pits of exhaustion. As if he almost didn't know how he'd continued living for so long.

Kristopher kneeled before her, taking her hand before planting a kiss on her knuckles.

Nolia's cousins, Cathrinus and Caius, moved from their seats as if to follow their father's lead, but Nolia held up her free hand.

"There's no need for so much formality," she said.

The boys' dark skinned faces stared at her as if in surprise before one broke out into a grin.

"So you're still our little Nolia?" Cathrinus asked.

"Nolia is queen," Kristopher reminded him as he stood. "We'll give her the respect she deserves."

The staff had laid out a bright white cloth on the table with gold plates, chalices, and cutlery. The table was otherwise empty, but the moment Nolia was seated, servants burst through the staff door, offering a variety of drinks for them to choose from while others placed the first course, a pesto toast sprinkled with cheese, on a smaller gold plate on top of the ones already in front of them.

"I'm sure you remember my wife," Caius said once their drinks had been poured.

Nolia nodded, taking a sip of the sweet raspberry wine she'd picked. "Ingrid," she said, looking at the pale young woman with long blonde hair and blue eyes. "I haven't seen you since your wedding. You haven't visited the palace." She glanced at the other members of her extended family. "Although I suppose none of you have visited recently."

"We've wanted to," Kristopher told her. "But we haven't wanted to travel since Ophelia became pregnant."

Nolia's eyes trailed to her uncle's new wife, a woman with hazel eyes, curly black hair, and dark skin. They'd been married after Caius and Ingrid in a surprise ceremony that neither Nolia nor Katrine had attended. She hadn't understood the secrecy or the rush until the pregnancy was announced.

In Ophelia's arms was a small bundle, and it wasn't until it moved that Nolia realized it was a baby. It was Katiana. Her *heir*.

"We haven't introduced you to your newest cousin," Kristopher realized, standing to take her from Ophelia. "Would you like to hold her?"

Panic rushed through Nolia's veins. She didn't know anything about babies; she didn't think she'd ever spent time with one. Occasionally the nobles at court would bring their children, but they were never as small as Katiana was.

"I'll show you how," Kristopher assured her as he brought the newborn to her. "All you have to do is support her head."

Nolia allowed him to place Katiana in her arms, and she peered down at the baby's scrunched up face. Corinne had told her that from the moment she'd held Nolia, she could tell she would take after Katrine, but Nolia didn't see the same with Katiana. She didn't think the baby looked like much of a person yet.

"We named her Katiana in honor of your mother," Kristopher said, leaning over to adjust the blanket. "We considered Katrine, but you know your mother forbade us from giving any possible daughters her name. She wanted to be the only Katrine in our family, and I figured that her death wouldn't redact that order."

"I told him Katiana was the better option anyway considering your mother executed the only family member who named their daughter Katrine," Cathrinus added. When Nolia blinked at him, he elaborated, "Miri? You know that her oldest was named Katrine, don't you?"

"Yes." Nolia quickly glanced back down at the baby. She'd always avoided using Miri's daughter's names. Having names made them more real to her, making their deaths by her mother's hand more tragic.

There was a moment of awkward silence before Nolia handed Katiana back to her father.

"Did Uncle Thiodore tell you why I requested your presence?" she asked, picking up her slice of toast.

Kristopher nodded, returning to his seat on Nolia's right. When Ophelia reached for the baby, he refused, pulling Katiana closer to him. "Your father didn't have my support when he tried to take the throne, and never was going to," he said. "He promised that he'd let us be if I agreed to a betrothal between Katiana and Alaric, and so I did."

"We wanted to fight," Caius added, shooting a pointed look in Ophelia's direction.

Ophelia didn't shrink away from his stare, her expression hardening instead. "I refused to put my days-old child at risk like that," she spoke for the first time.

"I understand," Nolia said, nibbling on her toast. "As my heir, Katiana will require extra protection, and I intend to provide it."

"But Katiana will not always be the next person in line for the throne."

Nolia stopped mid-bite to stare at Ophelia, who tore her daughter out of Kristopher's arms.

"Unless this is Your Majesty's way of telling us you won't be having children?"

The food became less appetizing as Nolia's stomach churned. She'd never admitted it to anyone, but she'd always been afraid that she would struggle to fall pregnant like Katrine had. No one had ever commented that she may face the same issue, but it had haunted the back of her mind as the time came closer for the Competition. She didn't want to face the same criticism and shame her mother had.

But Nolia also didn't want to alienate her heir to the point of having to execute her either.

"I have some time before I marry and—"

The doors flew open, and Nolia nearly shrieked.

"Isiris?" Kristopher dropped his toast.

"My favorite cousin," Isiris replied, striding in with her son on her heels. "Having a feast with my beautiful daughter-in-law who didn't think to invite me or her fiancé."

"Fiancé?!" everyone echoed.

Isidore's face was the brightest shade of red Nolia had ever seen, and he stared at her with pleading eyes.

"I don't know why you would want to be included," Nolia answered with a glare. "Especially when I gave you an incredibly important task."

"A task we've already finished," Isiris replied. "And we're famished. Aren't we, my sweet boy?"

Isidore blushed brighter.

Nolia sighed, turning her glare on the guards who'd let Isiris in and motioning for them to close the door. Then she looked at the servants, who hustled into the kitchen to get plates for Isiris and Isidore as well as bring out the second course.

They were set up on Kristopher and Ophelia's side of the table, and Kristopher stared at them wide-eyed the entire time, as if he couldn't believe it was his cousin.

"So what fascinating conversation did we interrupt?" Isiris asked, biting into the salmon benedict that Nolia's cook had swiftly prepared when the feast had become a brunch.

"The wedding," Cathrinus quickly said, glancing between Nolia and Isidore. "Nolia was saying that she wasn't going to be married anytime soon."

"Nonsense," Isiris answered, shooting Nolia a disapproving look. "Icaria doesn't have time to wait. Queens are always married with an heir on the sidelines, ready to step in should they be needed. Katrine ascended childless, and that caused a great deal of upheaval. Nolia will have no choice but to do the same, but the wedding can't be too long afterwards if we want to bring Icaria into an age of long-awaited peace."

"It's rather ironic that a rebel would speak about wanting peace," Nolia commented, and Ophelia gasped, scooting away from Isiris. Isiris only grinned back at her. "Besides," Nolia said, "even if I don't have a husband or a child when I'm crowned, I'll have an heir." She motioned towards Katiana. "She'll be raised as such until I have a daughter."

"You're going to set up a royal nursery at...?" Isiris paused, looking at Kristopher. "I'm afraid I haven't kept good tabs on you and Thio. Are you still living at Anitola?"

Kristopher nodded; at his first wedding, Katrine had gifted Kristopher and his family the right to live at the eastern palace. "I'm afraid I haven't kept tabs on you at all since you disappeared. Not for lack of trying."

Nolia would have allowed them a sweeter reunion if Isiris hadn't shown up uninvited. So instead, she got the conversation back on track.

"I'd like for the royal nursery to be set up here at Candicia."

This time Kristopher dropped his fork. "Royal children are always sent to one of the other palaces until they reach school age," he said. "It would be perfectly normal for her to be raised at Anitola with us, if that's what you're concerned about."

"That's not where my concern lies," Nolia replied, finally taking a bite of her salmon. Almost everyone else was nearly done with theirs. "I'll appear stronger if I embrace the heir that I do have and keep her nearby, unlike... my mother's method."

Ophelia's eyes widened as she stared at her baby, who was surprisingly calm despite all of the noise they were making. "You brought us here with the intention of stealing our daughter?"

"Your daughter is not yours," Isiris answered sharply. "She's Icaria's heir, and the queen can do with her whatever she likes, as the previous one did with my sister and nieces. If that displeases you, perhaps you should have thought twice about who you were sleeping with before you fell pregnant."

Everyone stared at her, dumbfounded by the veracity of her words, but Nolia was most shocked that Isiris had come so quickly to her defense. Especially when they'd just been arguing over her not wanting to marry her son.

Ophelia's face twisted into a scowl, but Nolia cleared her throat before she could speak.

"Exactly," she said. "I'll keep Katiana here with me until I have a daughter, but it isn't as if I'll be keeping her from you. You'll be welcome to live here with her." Nolia tried to smile. "It may be nice to have family around."

"Yes," Isidore quickly agreed, raising a glass to Cathrinus and Caius. "I had no idea I had cousins around my age, and I'm eager to get to know you."

"So it's decided," Nolia said, ignoring the tension in the air as she nodded to the servants. "Let's have dessert now. My cook makes a delicious coffee cake."

11

Audrie

AUDRIE STAYED BY Levi's side like Mikael stayed by Cilia's until they were forced to part ways. Neither set had been given guards to follow them since they needed to be questioned first, and it made Audrie oddly uncomfortable. She'd been wanting to ditch them from the moment she'd arrived at Candicia, but now she was wishing they'd come back. She didn't feel safe without them.

At least she had Mikael if anything happened.

"You've been quiet this morning," Mikael commented as they turned a corner. He'd assured her that he knew the way back to the knights' dormitories, and Audrie hadn't argued the matter.

"I suppose." Audrie glanced down at her feet, peeking out from the blue dress she'd picked out that morning from her own wardrobe. It was too simple with its laced bodice to be from the queen's closet, but she liked it, nonetheless.

"What's on your mind?"

Audrie scowled, knowing better than to admit what had her full concentration: Darius. She'd been trying not to think about him, especially after letting Lia go to wherever Meriah was keeping him. Yet she worried about today being the third day of his kidnapping. If Lia didn't arrive in time, would Meriah do something to him?

"Audrie?" Mikael asked.

Audrie swallowed, shoving thoughts of Darius away as she scrambled to find something else to talk about. Something that would capture Mikael's attention.

"What is it about Yadira that caught your eye?"

Mikael grimaced at the question; not quite the reaction Audrie had been expecting. Still, she barreled on.

"Let me guess. It was her hair, right? Auburn's a rather pretty color. Or..." Audrie paused, realizing too late that it wasn't the best game to play when there wasn't much she liked about Yadira. "It wouldn't be her status since she isn't technically noble," she finally said. "I'm also not sure if she's still a lady-in-waiting after accidentally letting Nolia escape from the tower."

"Yes, to find *you*," Mikael answered, raising his eyebrows at her.

"Yadira told you about that?"

"No, Nolia did. When it was the two of us."

There was something wistful about his tone that made Audrie look at him more carefully. "We haven't spoken about that," she said. "Nolia didn't give me many details aside from finding Calix, and later Isiris' camp. But I'm sure more happened before that."

Mikael stopped mid-step. "Are you trying to insinuate something? Because let me make myself very clear: I was nothing but a gentleman to my queen, and if I hadn't been, do you think I'd be here?"

"That's not what I meant," Audrie said quickly. She would have never admitted it, but it was slightly terrifying whenever Mikael raised his voice when he normally was so friendly. "I was saying that you two are close now. If she lets you call her by her first name, she must have started liking you during that time."

Mikael's face grew red, and Audrie almost asked what she'd said wrong before he blurted out, "Nolia is engaged. She doesn't like me."

Audrie blinked. "I didn't mean that sort of 'like,'" she answered. "Why would you assume I did?"

"No reason."

Mikael hurried away from her, but Audrie remained still, staring intently at the back of his head before the realization pierced her like a dagger. "Mikael, no!" she gasped, chasing after him.

"I haven't done anything wrong," Mikael swiftly answered.

"Nothing wrong?" Audrie repeated, struggling to keep up. "She's my best friend, and I trusted you with her. How could you —?"

"How could I *not*?"

Mikael stopped again, and Audrie ran into his back, but it didn't faze him as he turned to grab her shoulders, steadying her.

"When I asked about her, you told me she was your favorite person in the world," Mikael said. "Is it so difficult to believe that someone else may find wonderful qualities about her too?"

"That's different." Audrie slapped his hands away. "Nolia and I have known each other since we were babies, since before we understood the concept of princess and peasant. I didn't befriend her because I wanted something from her, I just liked her. You, on the other hand, only had the intention of coming into her life to *win* her."

Mikael flinched. "That's not true," he argued. "I wanted to help you save her, and you can't pretend you would have succeeded without me."

"Maybe not," Audrie said. "But that doesn't change the fact that you competed."

"I told you I came to the Competition because of my—"

"Your dream sent by the gods? You sincerely think you're special enough for them to reach out to you?" Audrie mocked, and when hurt flashed across his features, she knew that she should stop, but the words continued to pour out of her. "You may have convinced yourself that you didn't want to be king, but I remember what you asked when we met. If there was anything I wanted to do as king. You wouldn't have been curious about that if you weren't already daydreaming about the throne, about what you wanted to do the second you forced Nolia into marriage."

"I would never force anyone to do anything," Mikael told her. "What kind of person do you think I am?"

"Apparently the kind who takes advantage of people's trust," Audrie answered. "I trusted you to keep her safe when I couldn't. Instead you went ahead and..." She didn't know how to finish her sentence. She was clueless as to how to describe how badly of a betrayal she felt this was.

"I can't help that I developed feelings for her." Mikael avoided her eyes as he spoke. "I sincerely never meant to. I only wanted to bring Nolia back to Candicia."

Audrie shook her head. "Then what happened?"

Mikael hesitated before admitting, "I won't deny that her beauty didn't make it easier. But I also admired her loyalty towards you, and her sense of duty to Icaria. She was so kind and thoughtful with me, even when she had every reason not to be. She was... better than I could have ever imagined."

The affection in his tone almost made Audrie want to smack some sense into him. To her, it didn't sound like enough for him to suddenly fall madly in love with Nolia. But then again, he'd never actually said that he *loved* her, had he?

"Does she know?" Audrie asked.

"Of course not," Mikael said quickly. "And you're not going to tell her."

Yeah, right. Audrie crossed her arms. Nolia deserved to know. If at the very least to spare Mikael's feelings. Audrie needed to warn her best friend not to do anything to lead him on.

"You're in no place to be making demands," Audrie told him.

"It's not a demand, it's a request," Mikael said. "An incredibly reasonable one. I don't want to ruin the friendship that we've developed over this. I want her to feel as if she can depend on me, like she did now, asking me to interrogate the knights. She doesn't need to know about my silly little feelings."

Audrie paused, searching his face. "Is that all they are?" she asked. "Silly little feelings?"

Mikael smiled, his jade green eyes remaining empty. "It's what they have to be. She's engaged to someone else."

"Someone that she's not in love with," Audrie felt the need to point out, and Mikael only shook his head.

"Perhaps not now, but I've seen her with Isidore," he said, motioning for Audrie to keep walking. "He's proven that he's a good person to her. He reins Isiris in and exposed Calix's true colors. He agreed to marry Nolia to save her."

"Nolia was never looking for someone to save her," Audrie responded, following him. "You do realize that, don't you?"

"Do *you* realize that?" Mikael asked. "You were the one who pretended to be a boy and put down the money for two tickets to the mainland. You wanted to 'save' her from the Competition and her fate as Icaria's queen."

My intentions were noble! she wanted to snap, but bit down on her tongue. Levi had told her she was being selfish before she left for the Competition, and she knew Mikael agreed.

So instead, Audrie told him, "I'm her best friend, and you're a boy."

"I'm her friend," Mikael said as if it were the worst thing to be.

Audrie stared at him as they inched closer to where the knights were staying. "Yadira," she finally said. "You never told me what you liked about her."

Mikael gave her a tired look. "Isn't it obvious? I didn't choose to court her. Nolia decided it."

• • •

Audrie hadn't known what to expect when it came to interviewing the knights, but she certainly hadn't thought it would be quite so boring. She'd been locked in a room talking to them for hours, learning absolutely nothing aside from the fact that the boys wanted to go home. They complained that the guards watching over them weren't nice enough—and since they were still there, Audrie sent Nolia a note telling her they needed to be questioned by Alexie's soldiers too.

But their complaints didn't stop there. They complained that the food wasn't as good as it had been during the Competition; they complained that they had nothing to do besides play card games or talk to each other; and they complained that they hadn't heard from their families in days.

That last complaint was a genuine one in Audrie's eyes, and something she intended to do something about. She simply didn't know what could be done when Candicia was under lockdown.

"Are you listening to me?"

Naturally Audrie wasn't, but she nodded at the boy seated in front of her. She and Mikael had set up their interrogation spots inside two knightless bedrooms next to each other.

The rooms were furnished with three beds, wardrobes, and a desk to share. Whenever a new boy walked in, Audrie signaled for the boys to sit in the bedroom's middle bed while she remained either on the desk chair or pacing in front of them. Some were more nervous than others, but she'd come across quite a few boys who'd only been angry. Much like the one in front of her now.

"Of course I'm listening," Audrie said as she shifted in the chair and glanced outside the doorless room. The knights' guards had swiftly lined the boys up, and it wasn't getting any shorter. At this rate, she and Mikael would be there all day, and she was starting to get hungry.

"What did I just say?"

Audrie turned back at the boy. "It honestly doesn't matter to me. You've already proven you're loyal to Her Majesty."

"That feels ironic considering you're her biggest threat," the boy replied. "You're the girl who pretended to be a knight to stop the Competition, aren't you?"

For a moment, Audrie wondered how far gossip about her had reached. It was possible everyone in Icaria had heard some form of the story by now, especially since there had been soldiers searching for her and Nolia. In Elias' version, she'd been a spy who kidnapped his daughter, and she had a feeling that was what the knights had been told as well.

"Audrie."

She was proud of herself not for jumping as she turned towards the doorway. Mikael hovered inside, with a face she hadn't been expecting.

"Rubin ended up in my line," Mikael said, motioning towards the red haired boy. "He had some questions that I knew you would be able to answer."

Rubin was dressed in the same bright yellow shirt with worn out shoes that she'd seen him in last. His body had filled out, plumper due to the regular meals he was receiving at the palace. Any other boy likely would have been happy with his current circumstances, but Audrie could tell he was miserable. It made her all the less excited to see him again.

"Go," Audrie told the boy sitting across from her. "You may be loyal to the queen, but I'd watch how you speak to those closest to her if you ever want to go home."

"There's no plans to let us leave?" Rubin asked once the boy had slipped out.

"Not that I'm aware of," Mikael admitted as he moved to sit on the bed closest to the door. "Unless Her Majesty told Audrie something differently?"

"I'm sure she'll let you go once she's sussed out any possible Elias sympathizers," Audrie answered. "Are you going to sit?"

"No," Rubin said, taking a couple of steps from the doorway before crossing his arms. "I want to know where Darius is. I haven't heard from him since he told me he got out of the dungeon. He wasn't sure if he'd be allowed to leave, but said he'd keep writing to me so long as he was here."

"He wrote to you?" Audrie asked, sharper than she meant to.

"He said it was the first thing he asked if he could do."

Audrie sank down in her chair, her face growing warm with anger. *Rubin was the first thing on Darius' mind when he left the dungeon*, she thought. So how had he seen no issue with kissing her at most an hour or two later?

"Did he tell you anything else?" Mikael asked, raising his eyebrows at Audrie before glancing at Rubin.

He shook his head. "I'm learning how to read, so he couldn't tell me anything too complicated."

Audrie was incredibly close to making a rude comment about *that*, but somehow kept her mouth shut. It wasn't Rubin's fault no one had taught him, and besides, he wasn't the person she was actually upset with.

"Audrie was with him last," Mikael commented, eyeing her. "I saw him at the coronation, and it looked like he followed you out."

"He did," Audrie said begrudgingly. "We were caught and separated again almost immediately after."

"So you don't know where he is either?" Rubin asked, his shoulders slouching.

"Actually... I sort of do."

"What do you mean by 'sort of?'"

Audrie sighed, trying not to let either boy see her panic. "He'll be back soon, there's no need to—"

"Where did he go?" Rubin interrupted, taking a step closer to her, and making Mikael sit up, as if he expected him to attack her.

"He's with some former spies of Elias," Audrie said carefully. "They're not going to kill him, he's just... leverage."

"Leverage?" Rubin and Mikael echoed.

Audrie bit her lip. "Some spies agreed to work with Nolia to expose what her father was up to, but they wanted some sort of reassurance that nothing would happen to them. They took Darius in order to ensure that."

"You used him as some sort of bargaining chip?" Rubin burst out, his face nearly as red as his hair.

"It wasn't my choice," Audrie objected. "They picked him."

"Why him?"

Audrie shrugged, trying to come up with a good answer. It wasn't as if she could tell him the truth. *Or maybe you should*, the thought pricked her mind. Didn't Rubin deserve to know what his boyfriend had been up to behind his back?

Audrie squashed the idea before it could grow into a beast. She knew she didn't want to tell Rubin because she cared about him. She only cared about herself, and she was the one who'd allowed herself to play with fire.

"It makes sense they would target him," Mikael commented. "He's not a member of the Girard family, so wasn't under as close guard as they were. It was easier to kidnap him."

"Exactly," Audrie said, smiling with relief.

Rubin relaxed. "You freed him when I asked too, so they must have assumed you cared about him."

Mikael's head shot back to Audrie, but Rubin was speaking again before he could open his mouth.

"What are you doing to rescue him?"

Nothing, Audrie almost said. She may have done what Meriah asked and sent Lia to her, but *she* certainly hadn't been doing anything.

Instead of answering the question, Audrie replied, "He'll be back soon. I'll send him running into your arms the moment he returns."

Rubin's cheeks pinked, and Mikael raised his eyebrows, clearing his throat.

"I don't know what Darius told you," Rubin said stiffly, "but whatever is going on between the two of us should remain between the two of us."

"Of course it does," Audrie lied, and Rubin seemed to know she was.

"I'll be waiting for him." He nodded to her before giving Mikael his thanks and darting out of the room.

"You already questioned him?" Audrie confirmed.

"Yes." Mikael stood. "Although now I think I may need to question *you*."

A tap on the doorway came to Audrie's rescue.

"Lady Audrie?"

It was a guard that Audrie found slightly familiar, likely one of the many of Nolia's that followed the queen around.

"Her Majesty asked that I get you."

Mikael frowned, clearly displeased. "Only Audrie?"

"Yes." The guard motioned out the door. "Please, Lady Audrie, Her Majesty was in a panic."

"Oh my gods, what could have happened?" Audrie mumbled before she told Mikael that she'd be back as soon as possible.

"Let her know that whatever it is, I offer my assistance as well," was all he replied.

Audrie and the guard raced out of the knights' dormitories. She felt bad for abandoning Mikael with the never-ending line of boys, but it wasn't as if she had a choice in the matter. Nolia needed her, and it didn't matter to her if she was asking for Audrie as her queen or as her best friend. She'd be there for her either way.

"This way, Lady Audrie."

The guard remained by her side as they hurried along. Eventually he took her arm to make it easier when they veered down different hallways. She realized, after some twists, that he wasn't steering her towards the throne room like she'd expected. Audrie figured Nolia must have moved to take care of some other sort of business that had her so alarmed.

"You don't technically have to call me 'lady' by the way," Audrie said, nearly out of breath even though they were going at her speed.

"As her best friend, you'll be a lady soon enough," the guard responded. "Although as her half sister trying to steal her throne, it may be a bad idea to give you a title."

Too late Audrie realized that the guard had led her down a dead end. She turned towards him, prepared to fight with only her fists despite the sword she knew was at his side, but she didn't get the chance to hit him. He swung the hilt of his sword at her head, sending her crashing down onto the cold, hard floor and making everything go dark.

12

Nolia

DESPITE RESERVATIONS REGARDING the matter, Nolia interrogated the nobles who'd supported Elias. It went better than she could have expected, with most pleading that they'd had no other choice if they'd wanted to keep their lives, and Nolia was exhausted by the end of the day. All she wanted was to read the titleless blue book that she'd found on Katrine's nightstand. But Yadira wouldn't stop talking about Cilia, and the last thing that Nolia wanted was to hear about how well she was getting along with Mikael's sister.

Nolia was glad when Isidore appeared to speak with her, shooing Yadira off the couch they'd settled into in the tea room, and ushering Isidore onto it instead.

Isidore sat on the far end, appearing uncomfortable, but not allowing it to stop him from his purpose for being there. "I wanted to reassure you that my mother wasn't lying about how our interrogations went," he said. "As well as apologize."

"Apologize?" Nolia repeated.

Before Isidore could open his mouth, there was a tap on the doorway of the tea room and Giana, the only other person left in the room, stepped out of the way for another guard.

"Your Majesty." He bowed. "Lord Levi is at the door, asking to speak with his sister, Lady Audrie."

QUEENLY

Nolia almost snorted. The staff had taken it upon themselves to refer to Audrie and Levi as nobles, and she had yet to correct them. She knew her best friend would love being referred to so formally, but she wasn't sure Levi would feel the same way. He'd likely already scolded them about using it incorrectly.

"You can let him know that Audrie isn't here," Nolia replied. "She should be sleeping in her own room tonight."

The guard nodded before bowing and exiting.

"You were saying?" Nolia turned back to Isidore.

"I..." He cleared his throat. "I only wanted to apologize for my mother's behavior earlier with your uncle."

Nolia shrugged. "Aside from her meddlesome nature, I'm sure she was excited to see him after so many years."

Isidore glanced down. "I also wanted to say that I haven't encouraged her insistence on setting a wedding date. We don't have to rush into marriage."

Relief swept over Nolia, even as she bit her lip. "You do understand my hesitance, don't you? It doesn't have anything to do with you, I—"

"I'm aware that your heart is elsewhere, Your Majesty."

Nolia felt as if he'd kicked her in the stomach. "What?"

Isidore gave her a sad smile. "You need time to mourn the relationship you thought you'd had, and I can't blame you for that."

"You can't?" Nolia parroted back, her eyes wide.

"No," Isidore said with a shrug. "Regardless of my opinion on the matter, His Majesty picked the perfect boy for you."

The perfect boy for me? Nolia set her book down before she could drop it. She'd been afraid of having Elias in charge of her Competition since it meant he was practically choosing her husband for her. She'd insisted to Katrine that he would pick someone as terrible as he was, to which her mother had only scoffed at. Now Nolia was wondering if Katrine had been right not to be so worried. Elias may not have set up the trials to find her a husband, instead wanting to find boys for his army, but he'd always intended there to be a clear winner. And that winner, the first boy to make it to the

111

tower, the one who'd passed Elias' trials with flying colors, had been Mikael.

Mikael. A boy not horrible at all like her father.

"He knew that Calix would have the charm to win you over."

It was as if Isidore had knocked the air out of her again. "Calix?" Nolia blurted out. "You think that my heart is with him?!"

"Of course." Isidore appeared wary by her outburst. "Who else could it...?" His expression changed, understanding dawning as he quickly stood. "I'm sorry, Your Majesty, I'm afraid I've overstepped. This isn't a conversation we should be having."

"I suppose not," Nolia mumbled, too panicked to say anything differently.

"I'm sorry," Isidore said again before bowing.

Nolia didn't watch him leave. Instead she stared at the ring he'd given her that hung from her neck. The promise of the marriage that Nolia already feared would be as loveless as that of Elias and Katrine's.

• • •

"Your Majesty, wake up."

Nolia turned towards the familiar voice, her eyes still shut as she pulled the covers over her head.

"Your Majesty?"

"Not now, Corinne," Nolia answered.

"Nolia... Corinne is no longer with us, remember?"

Nolia opened her eyes, bringing the blankets down below her chin. She blinked at the girl hovering above her, the darkness of the room making it difficult for her eyes to focus.

"Giana?" she asked. "What are you doing in my room in the middle of the night?"

"Your presence has been requested," Giana answered.

"Not at this hour it hasn't," Nolia said, tempted to roll over again.

"It's urgent, and we aren't sure what to do."

Nolia groaned. "What is it?"

"Justina is here," Giana told her.

"Justina?" Nolia was suddenly wide awake. "The rebel?"

Giana nodded.

"But I didn't send an envoy to Dismund," Nolia said, rubbing her eyes as she sat up. "Or did I? I'm fairly certain my council and I agreed that we wouldn't meet with her without being sure of where her loyalties lie."

"That's what you decided," Giana agreed, "but Justina has taken matters into her own hands. She arrived not all that long ago, demanding to speak with you."

"She never did something like this with Katrine," Nolia mumbled. "Does she think she can get away with it with me?"

Giana shrugged helplessly. "What should we do, Your Majesty?"

"Well... I can't show her that I'll come running the moment she wants my presence," Nolia said slowly. "She should wait until a more reasonable hour."

"So should we put her in the dungeon?" Giana asked.

Nolia shut her eyes, debating her response.

"Don't tell me you fell asleep again?"

"No." Nolia quickly opened her eyes. "Keep her in one of our guest rooms under careful surveillance. She'll be a guest, albeit an uninvited one, until she proves herself an enemy."

"Yes, Your Majesty." Giana headed towards the door.

"Tell Isiris," Nolia called after her. "Not right now, but whenever she wakes. I want her with me to talk to that rebel."

• • •

Nolia chose a silver tiara with amethysts that she'd seen Katrine wear on a few occasions. She figured that now more than ever was the right moment to wear Icaria's royal color, even if the gown she'd picked was made of a shimmering silver. Nolia had liked the way it made the purple of the jewels pop more, but almost immediately regretted the decision when she saw Isiris.

The rebel wore purple from head to toe. As someone of royal blood, she was allowed to wear the color at court, but it felt odd seeing her in it. Isiris normally tended to pick black.

"This is utterly ridiculous," Isiris grouched as they made their way to the throne room. "We shouldn't be meeting with her at all. She should have been sent to the dungeon the moment you heard she'd broken into the palace."

"She didn't break in," Nolia objected.

"She came here uninvited and without warning."

"What can I say? She's desperate to speak with me," Nolia said. "Much more desperate than she was with my mother."

Isiris snorted. "She's not desperate; she's calculating. You're young and came to the throne unexpectedly. She thinks that she can manipulate you."

Nolia had the same fear herself. Justina would have never attempted to enter the palace if Katrine were on the throne, and was only doing so now because she thought Nolia would let her get away with it—which she wouldn't. Whatever Justina wanted from her wouldn't easily be handed over.

"Your Majesty." Nolia could hear the guard's voice, but she couldn't see her behind the other guards flanked around her. "Lord Levi is looking for you."

Nolia frowned. It was rather early for him to be awake, but perhaps this was normally what time he woke up to get started on his chores at Dismund. "Let him know that I'm in a meeting, but I'll see him after."

She didn't have a chance to wonder what Levi may want because Isiris was already grumbling more complaints under her breath.

"Justina may be calculating, but I think she's desperate," Nolia told her. "She wanted my attention badly enough to risk her freedom."

"Or perhaps she knew you wouldn't lock her away," Isiris said with a disapproving stare. It reminded Nolia of the look Corinne would give her when she was misbehaving.

"I'm going to hear her out before I decide anything," Nolia told her. "Katrine strived to quell rebellions peacefully, and I'll do the same."

"Look how that turned out," Isiris grumbled.

Before Nolia could scold her for speaking so unkindly about her mother, they'd arrived at the throne room doors. The guards confirmed that Justina was already inside before they opened the doors and announced their presence.

"Kneel before Queen Nolia Riona of Icaria, accompanied by Isiris Riona."

Nolia kept her head up high as she strode down the purple carpet, passing Justina without a glance before she climbed up onto the tallest platform where her mother's throne was under a golden canopy.

Nolia settled into it, her skin crawling as she met Justina's stare.

Justina was a tall woman with sunburned skin, dirty blonde hair, and blue eyes. She smiled at Nolia, her face wrinkling.

"Queen Nolia," she said in a deep tone.

Nolia didn't have the chance to open her mouth before Isiris was snapping, "You don't speak to the queen unless spoken to."

"I'd assumed that was why I was here," Justina answered, glaring at her. Isiris had placed herself at the bottom of the platform to Nolia's left. "It certainly wasn't to see you again."

"You two know each other," Nolia realized, tempted to glare at Isiris too.

"Yes, Your Majesty," Justina said. "I'm surprised your aunt didn't mention it."

"We've been dealing with more important matters," Isiris replied.

"Then I suppose I did the right thing by coming here instead of waiting another time for an envoy."

Nolia frowned. "If I were truly interested, I could have spared someone."

"Perhaps," Justina agreed. "Although I think you would have sent me to be executed along with your father if you were uninterested in what I have to say."

"I think of myself as someone who will always help those in need," Nolia said. "So whatever it is that has you distressed enough to come to me personally, I will hear out. Even if you are one of Icaria's guiltiest people."

"So is your aunt, and she seems to be freely roaming Candicia," Justina pointed out.

"You and I are not the same," Isiris snapped.

"Aren't we?" Justina raised an eyebrow at her. "Don't we both want the same thing for our country?"

"No," Isiris answered. "You refused Elias' invitations to work under him because it wasn't about exchanging a queen for anyone else. You wanted the monarchy gone altogether."

"Untrue," Justina said, a smile returning to her face as she looked at Nolia. "I always looked forward to the day when Icaria would be under the rule of a new queen."

There was something malicious in her eyes that made Nolia clutch the arms of her throne. "Interesting that you would so blatantly admit to being eager for my mother's death."

"I'm only being honest," Justina said with a shrug. "Icaria was not thriving under her rule. It was time for someone new to come to power."

And you think the queendom will thrive under me? Nolia wanted to ask. She'd wondered about it often herself, particularly during the Competition. That was when she'd found out how little those closest to her believed in her capability as queen, Audrie included. It was a sting she hoped would dull once she'd proved them wrong. Assuming she ever was able to.

"Why are you here?" Nolia asked, deciding not to play any more games with the rebel. "I have more important matters to attend to."

Justina shifted on her knee, and Nolia knew it was likely starting to hurt. "I wish to work with you, Your Majesty. Just as I tried time and time again with Queen Katrine. I thought that I'd made that clear in my letter."

Nolia had reread the letter that morning, but she didn't mention that. Instead she replied, "What makes you think we can work together? You're Icaria's most infamous rebel and I'm the queen."

"Rebels are the reason you have your throne at all," Justina pointed out, nodding to Isiris. "Isiris, more than any of us, had good reason to oppose your family's rule, and she could have killed you, but she didn't. There was something about you that convinced her there was a reason worth saving the Rionas."

Yes, the idea of her son in that chair next to me, Nolia thought, glancing at the king's empty throne. Corinne's voice drifted through the back of her mind, asking if perhaps she should have allowed Isidore to join their meeting. She ignored it, remembering the way he'd looked at her the night before. He knew where her heart was, and until she contained it, she would be avoiding both him and Mikael.

"That's why I'm so eager to offer you my assistance," Justina said. "You're a queen who can win over those who would normally oppose her, and I want to be a part of that."

"Wait." Nolia blinked at her. "Are you saying that you think you can convince other rebels to join my side?"

"You've forgotten that most rebellions were orchestrated by her father," Isiris commented. "The people who partook in those weren't really rebels, they just needed the extra coin in their pocket."

"Yes, but not everyone was a paid lackey of his," Justina said. "Many groups like yours originated on their own, and only accepted his help when they ran out of money."

Isiris crossed her arms. "Is *that* why you're truly here? You've run out of whatever inheritance or stolen goods were funding your operations?"

Justina smirked. "No need to worry over that. I have enough to keep me going for some time."

Nolia wrapped her fingers on the throne, staring at the rebel with the malicious glint still in her eyes. "I'll need a concrete plan if you expect me to believe that you want to work for me."

"*With* you," Justina corrected, shifting the weight again on her knee. "And I merely wanted to suggest a summit between you and all of the other rebel leaders."

"A summit? With rebels?" Isiris scoffed.

"It would have to be very carefully arranged for the safety of everyone," Justina said quickly. "My contacts would be hesitant to come to Candicia—or wherever else you'd like to host the event—unless they were offered a ceasefire, like I ask for now. But I know that there are some who would jump at the chance to speak to their queen. Rebels want to make Icaria a better place as much as you do, Your Majesty. We simply have different ways of going about it."

Isiris snorted. "Yes, like trying to burn the queendom down."

Nolia ignored her as she considered Justina's suggestion. It was a dangerous one, but if she could somehow ensure her own safety then wouldn't it be a good idea? When Katrine had tasked her with putting down an imaginary uprising of Justina's, Corinne had told her to think about *what* it was about. Nolia had listed off reasons the rebels may have been upset, but hadn't had an exact answer. Now she could get that. She could possibly eradicate rebellions in Icaria altogether.

"How do I know that your suggestion comes from a place of sincerity?" Nolia wondered out loud. "Especially with the knowledge that you'd written to my father as recently as a couple of days ago?"

Justina didn't appear surprised by the question, smiling instead as if she'd expected it. "King Elias was not the monarch Icaria needed, nor did I agree with what he was doing on a personal level. If he had no sense of loyalty towards his own family, how could I ever respect him, much less work with him?" She paused before adding, "I wanted to tell Her Majesty about him. The countless meetings that I attempted to arrange weren't merely about working together. They were about exposing Elias for who he truly was. It isn't my fault she never accepted my assistance."

Just like how it won't be if you reject me too, Justina's eyes seemed to add warningly.

Nolia wrapped her fingers on the throne again. "I'll consider your offer. For the time being, you'll remain here as my guest."

The guards leaped into action, grabbing Justina to escort her out. Nolia expected to see panic brush across Justina's face. Instead, all she did was smirk again. As if she'd stolen a treasure straight from Nolia's palm.

Nolia tried to keep her expression stoic as she watched her leave, her mind swirling with questions. Perhaps keeping Justina around wasn't such a good idea after all.

Just as Nolia watched the doors closing, finally about to have the necessary space she needed from the rebel, a hand reached out to stop it.

"Nolia," Levi said, gasping for air as if he'd been running.

"Levi?" Nolia frowned, spotting Justina glancing over her shoulder at them curiously, so she quickly motioned him inside. Once the door was properly shut, she asked, "What are you doing here? I told that guard I'd see you later."

"It must be an issue all Girards have," Isiris commented disapprovingly. "Can't ever do what they're told."

"I know, I'm sorry." Levi was still out of breath as he approached the platform. "I couldn't wait, I've been up all night. I had a bad feeling yesterday, and then I spoke to Mikael and—"

"What sort of bad feeling?" Nolia interrupted, hating the jolt that ran through her at the mention of Mikael. "What's wrong?"

"It's Audrie." Levi's golden flecked eyes were wild, crazed with fear. "She's missing."

13

Audrie

AUDRIE'S HEAD WAS pounding. The pain was too much for her to be able to remember if it was as bad or worse than how she'd felt with her concussion. Something told her that it must be worse, *so* much worse, since another blow to the head was the last thing she needed. She wouldn't have been surprised if this time it did leave damage.

When Audrie managed to open her eyes, she expected to see a cell. Instead, she was in a bedroom.

The walls were unpainted, and the wooden planks didn't look as if they'd been properly sanded down either, likely meaning that a brush against one would end in splinters. There was a single window in the room that's green curtains were wide open, but all Audrie could see from it were the tops of trees.

The only piece of furniture in the room was the bed that Audrie had been tucked into with coarse white sheets. It had tall bed posts that would reach her chest if she were standing, and one of them had a chain locked onto it. The other end was on Audrie's left wrist.

Audrie lifted her hand so she could stare at it, the lock rattling as she turned it over. It had been latched on rather tightly, obviously meant to disbenefit her dominant hand.

How did they know I'm left-handed? Audrie wondered as she sat up to examine the chain. It was long enough that she could get up and walk around. Perhaps even long enough that she could get to the window and look for help. Assuming there was any in the area.

Footsteps outside of her door interrupted her plan, and Audrie plunged back under the itchy sheets, her head barely hitting the pillow as the door burst open.

"Don't bother pretending. I know you're awake."

The door slammed shut as her guest moved towards her.

Audrie dared to flutter her eyes open. A boy stood before her, his bright green eyes peering back at her. There was something about his dark hair and curve of his face that Audrie found familiar. She examined the rest of him, noting from his frame that he exercised often. Likely doing the drills required of the military.

Trying to memorize the faces of the palace guards she'd come across seemed to be helping her, after all.

"Calix."

The boy's face broke out into a grin. "It's nice to meet you," he said. "Officially, I mean. The last times I saw you hardly count, considering you were pretending to be your brother."

"Yes, this is an official introduction for both of us." Audrie held out a hand as if to shake his. "Because the last time I saw you, you were also pretending. You never cared about my best friend."

Calix flinched. "Are you hungry?" he asked, ignoring her comment as he approached her with a wooden bowl.

Audrie crossed her arms. "I'm in no mood to be poisoned."

The boy laughed. "So you're afraid of being poisoned too?" he commented. "An odd thing for best friends to have in common." He shoved the bowl into Audrie's lap despite her objections.

Audrie picked up the tiny wooden spoon inside of the bowl, swirling around the vegetables in the black sauce covering them. She had no way of knowing if it was poisoned and cursed herself for not asking Darius to teach her since he claimed to be an expert on the topic.

Darius. Audrie's heart pinched as she wondered whether or not he'd been safely returned to Candicia. *And Rubin*, she reminded herself. He was the person Darius truly cared for and wanted to be with. Not her—not that she'd ever wanted to be with him in the first place. His kiss was just confusing her into thinking differently, wasn't it?

"Neither one of you is very honest either," Calix said softly, snapping her out of her thoughts of Darius. "You pretended to be your brother while she pretended to keep her promise about our relationship remaining a secret."

Audrie rolled her eyes. "That's different."

"Is it?"

"I wasn't a spy using all of the information she told me about you for ulterior motives," Audrie said, drowning her vegetables in the sauce. "In fact, I was happy to pretend you didn't exist like Nolia did whenever she came to Dismund. I'm sure that's the real reason she never let you go with her. It would have ruined everything."

Calix seemed surprised by the force of her words before his gaze hardened. "As if you're one to talk about ruining things. Wasn't it you who wanted to stop the Competition? Wasn't it your stupid plan to run to the first place people would think to look for you? Wasn't it you who was named Nolia's rival for the throne?"

Audrie blanched. "How did you hear about that?" she asked before shaking her head. "How are you here at all? You were tied up last I heard."

"That was a couple of days ago," Calix replied. "Which is why I'm here trying to feed you an *unpoisoned* dinner."

Audrie ignored his emphasis, tempted to throw her vegetables at him. Instead she latched onto the word before it. *Dinner.* She stared out the window, the late evening light streaming in. She'd been unconscious for a few hours.

Audrie thought of her family. They'd surely realized she was missing by now, and the repercussions would be great. Cecily was already so distraught over losing Alaric that her condition may have worsened over learning about Audrie's disappearance. Levi would

QUEENLY

be driving himself mad searching for her, refusing to eat or sleep like he did when his horse, Blink, had run away. Josip would likely get violent, yelling and throwing things the longer they went without finding her.

And Nolia? Her best friend would tear the palace down stone by stone in her search.

Audrie needed to be freed before it came to that point.

"Where is here?" Audrie asked, staring out the window again. She was suddenly certain that the chain wouldn't be long enough to stand as close to it as Calix was now.

"Consider this one of His Majesty's safe havens," he answered. "You're as secure here as his allies are."

"How can I be safe with his allies?"

Calix gave her a questioning look. "Because you're his daughter," he said. "His only remaining heir."

"I'm not," Audrie snapped.

"You are," Calix said. "Why would His Majesty lie about who's going to inherit his throne after him?"

Because he's an idiot, Audrie would have told him if she didn't have the same question herself. It hadn't made any sense to claim to be her biological father, especially after so blatantly denying it when she saw him in the dungeon.

When Agnesia had pointed out that Elias couldn't kill his only remaining child, there had been a better option: Levi. He was trying to turn Icaria into a kingdom, and since he needed a male heir, it only made sense.

Except that no one would believe Levi was Elias' when he looks like Father, Audrie reminded herself.

"I'm not Elias' daughter," Audrie repeated, for her own sake as much as Calix's. "I was the best excuse for him to kill Nolia."

Calix flinched again. "He was handing you, his daughter's best friend, a great deal of power," he insisted. "Why would he do that if he weren't telling the truth?"

123

"How much power does a dead girl have?" Audrie answered. "I have a feeling he was going to kill me the second he got the chance. One last act of revenge against his daughter."

"What good would that do?" Calix asked. "He has no other children."

Audrie frowned, hating that he was right. He couldn't have been depending on Beatrix's child being his heir when he didn't believe her. There was also the fact that he'd married Cecily, so his and Beatrix's child would have been illegitimate and unable to inherit.

Perhaps it would have resulted in a repeat of his previous situation. Cecily would need to die like Katrine in order for him to marry the mother of his illegitimate child and heir. But would he go through the trouble if it were another girl like Nolia?

"Are you going to eat or not?"

Audrie's head was still whirling with questions, and she barely heard him. "Not anything you give me," she answered.

Calix rolled his eyes. "Why would I kill my girlfriend's best friend?"

"Your *fake* girlfriend's best friend," Audrie corrected. "And if you were willing to kill her, why wouldn't you be willing to kill me?"

"I didn't want her to die," Calix snapped.

"You never did anything to try to stop it."

A heavy silence fell between the two of them, and Audrie waited for him to meet her eyes, to tell her differently. That he'd had a plan all along like Audrie to get Nolia out safely. To spare Nolia's life in case Audrie hadn't been there.

But he remained quiet, and Audrie knew she had all the response she needed.

• • •

The hunger became too much, and eventually Audrie ate. She dozed in between bites, the darkening room not helping to keep her awake, but she didn't mind too much. Not when she needed to be fully rested if she ever wanted to make it out of wherever she was.

Audrie was chewing on a carrot, her bites so loud in her ears that she almost didn't hear the footsteps coming in her direction. It was too late to look, much less *feel* alive, before her door had been thrown open.

"I'm not done yet," Audrie said, her mouth full of carrots. "Come back later, Calix."

A chuckle answered her, one that didn't belong to Calix's voice.

Audrie scrambled to sit up, nearly spilling her bowl, as a light flickered on over her head and a woman came into sight, her blue eyes staring intently at her.

"Who are you?" Audrie demanded.

The woman smirked. "Straight to the point," she commented. "I can appreciate that, Audrie Casimir."

Audrie bristled at the use of Elias' surname on her. "Girard," she said through clenched teeth. "My name is Audrie Girard."

The woman nodded, approaching her bedpost. "Mine is Justina."

"Justina?" Audrie blurted out. She stared at the woman as if expecting her to glow or for lightning to flash outside or do anything to show she was Icaria's most infamous rebel.

Instead Justina only grinned at her. "I take it you've heard of me?"

Audrie didn't bother to hide how unimpressed she was by the rebel's appearance. "I'd have to be living under a rock not to have heard how annoying you are."

Justina laughed. "Annoying to Katrine maybe, but you won't have to worry about me," she said. "I'll retire once Icaria has its rightful monarch on the throne."

"And you think that's *Elias*?"

Justina laughed again.

"I thought you weren't working with him," Audrie went on. "My father told me that you've always turned down his offers. Was he lying to me?" She was unable to stop the crack in her voice, the hurt creeping through despite all her father had already done.

A malicious glint appeared in Justina's eyes that made Audrie want to shrink back. "He wasn't," she told her. "I had no interest in working for Elias or anyone else for that matter."

"Then why are you here now?"

Justina paused, wrapping her fingernails on the bedpost she was leaning against. "I suppose there isn't any harm in telling you," she said. "It isn't as if you're ever going to escape."

Audrie swallowed, tightening her grip on her bowl as if she could hurl it at her without consequences. She was glad now that she hadn't wasted possibly the only chance she would have of doing so on Calix.

Justina moved closer to her, leaning down as she hissed, "The answer is very simple, dear child. Your little friend shouldn't be queen like her mother and her mother and so on should never have been. Icaria has been ruled for years now by a family that should have never been placed on its throne. I intend to fix that immediately."

Audrie's heart pounded wildly, every beat raising a new question. What was Justina's issue with the Riona family? Why did she think none of them were fit to rule? Why did she believe Elias was what would mend everything she thought was broken in the queendom?

What did Justina think was broken?

Audrie stared at her, remembering what her father had told Nolia about Justina. He'd claimed to be glad they were never able to recruit Justina because her intentions were so unclear.

"What do you want?" Audrie asked, keeping her voice low. "What are you really after?"

Justina grinned. "*That* I will keep to myself."

"Why are you here?" Audrie pushed. "Why did you come talk to me in the middle of the night?"

"I wanted to meet you," Justina said, straightening, "before I left for Candicia."

Panic sent a tremble down Audrie's back. "You're going to the palace?"

"Of course," Justina replied, flouncing towards the door. "I thought I'd give your so-called queen a visit."

Audrie forced herself to her feet, her head spinning. "She didn't send anyone to meet with you for a reason," she told Justina. "Nolia doesn't want to work with you."

"I realize that, and it's a shame she didn't make things easier on me," Justina replied, her fingers on the doorknob as she shrugged. "But I'm getting into that palace one way or another."

14

Nolia

THE BOOK WAS heavy in Nolia's hands, and while she'd been intending to read the worn copy from her mother's nightstand, she was getting ready to fling it across the tea room at Isiris' head. And her aunt seemed to be well aware of her intentions.

"Nolia—" she began.

"What do you mean you haven't been looking for her?" Nolia all but shrieked.

"We're needed elsewhere," Isiris answered, calmly. "Or is keeping Justina imprisoned not important?"

"You don't need *all* of your rebels to do that," Nolia exclaimed.

Isiris tilted her head slightly. "I've been thinking, Your Majesty," she said, "and I don't believe we should be referred to as rebels anymore. We're essentially one of your personal armies now."

Nolia lifted the book again, and Isiris stepped further from her. "Isiris, that's not what we're talking about right now."

"Why not? Don't my people and I deserve respect after everything we've done for you? We should be created into official members of the royal guard so that we can reap the benefits that come with doing the job we're already doing."

Of course this is about money, Nolia thought, shaking her head. Soldiers did make quite a bit, but likely not as much as Isiris was thinking.

"Can we talk about that later?" she said. "Audrie is *missing*."

"Yes, your rival to the throne," Isiris said dryly. "So isn't it rather obvious she was kidnapped by supporters of your father?"

Nolia stiffened, glancing around the tea room at her guards. No one had brought up the possibility to her, but she wondered if it was what they'd been thinking all along.

"Did you think she'd run away?" Isiris asked.

"No." Nolia lowered the book. Audrie had only ever wanted to run away once, and that had been with *her*. "I'm afraid that people who think she's a threat kidnapped her."

"I see." Isiris nodded thoughtfully. "It's possible; there's always extremists on any side of a war."

"We're not at war."

"Aren't we?" Isiris replied, raising her eyebrows. "Simply because your father is locked away doesn't mean his supporters have disappeared."

Nolia rolled her eyes at her insinuation. "There's still people interrogating the guards," she argued.

"Yes, *my* people," Isiris answered, "because the rest are too busy searching for your little friend."

"Didn't you just say your people were too busy with Justina?"

"And didn't you point out that I don't need everyone for that?"

Nolia scowled. "Have you at least asked Justina about Audrie's disappearance?"

"Of course not," Isiris said, making a face. "I try not to speak to her unless I have no other choice."

"I wouldn't think that you'd need me to tell you that you should have," Nolia said before pausing as she considered her reaction. "What's your history with Justina? You didn't mention that you'd worked together."

"We didn't. We simply crossed paths and decided to be friendly. Katrine was an enemy to both of us at the time."

"You should have mentioned it." Nolia sat, setting the book aside.

Isiris ignored her invitation to do the same. "I didn't realize you needed more evidence than you already have to know Justina is untrustworthy."

"It's because she's untrustworthy that I find her arrival and Audrie's disappearance so suspicious," Nolia said. "Don't you?"

Isiris frowned, considering the question. "Do we know for certain what time Audrie disappeared?"

"Yes. Levi told me that it was when she and Mikael were with the knights."

"And I imagine you've already spoken to Mikael about the matter," Isiris said, rolling her eyes.

Nolia's stomach twisted at the mention of him. She *should* have spoken to Mikael by now, but she'd been stupidly avoiding him all because of her silly crush.

"Nolia?"

"No," Nolia said, her cheeks warming. "But I will."

This is for Audrie, Nolia told herself, resolving that there was no way out of seeing Mikael. And she would have to be alright with that, so long as it meant it would help them find her best friend.

Isiris raised her eyebrows. "Good. Leave Justina to me."

"You promise that you'll ask her about Audrie?" Nolia asked.

Isiris smiled, not very reassuringly. "I swear to your gods that I will."

• • •

Mikael wasn't in his room or interrogating the knights or even with Yadira, who was prancing around the gardens with Cilia. Nolia was tempted to give up until she found Alexie, who informed her that he'd gone with Levi to see Cecily and Josip.

That didn't make her any more eager to see him since the last thing she wanted was to be confronted by Audrie's parents about their daughter's whereabouts, but she couldn't avoid them too. Especially when they also may have had an idea of who'd taken Audrie.

That was what Nolia was trying to convince herself of until she entered Cecily and Josip's room to find everyone in a panic.

"Nolia?" the boys shouted while Cecily collapsed to kneel on the ground mumbling, "I had no idea, Your Majesty," over and over again.

"What's going on?" Nolia demanded.

"What are you doing here?" Levi answered. "How did you know?"

"How did I know?" Nolia repeated.

"It's *her* palace," Mikael said. "She can go wherever she pleases."

"But—"

"How did I know what, Levi?" Nolia stared between the three of them.

Mikael jumped to kneel, and Levi swiftly copied him.

"Is anyone going to answer me?" Nolia realized that they were all positioned outside of Josip's room, the door wide open. She'd found it quite interesting that Elias had purposely picked out a room with separate bedrooms for them, as if he couldn't stand the idea of the couple he'd set up sleeping in the same bed.

Nolia then thought of Mikael and Yadira, and hated herself for understanding.

"Josip," she called out. "It's rather rude of you not to greet your queen. Especially one who's so graciously kept you alive." Nolia had meant the last part as a joke, but the three on the floor cringed. "Seriously, what's going on?" she insisted.

"We came here to see if my parents knew anything about what may have happened to Audrie," Levi finally said. "As you can see, my mother came out of her room to speak to us, but my father..."

"He's been so upset with me, Your Majesty," Cecily said, raising her tear stained eyes to meet Nolia's. "He's hardly left his room the past few days; I didn't think anything of it."

Nolia's world began to spin. "He's not here, is he?"

Mikael spoke, but she couldn't comprehend his words. When she thought that she may fall over, he was suddenly at her side. She let him latch onto her arm for a moment, his warm fingers calming her, before she moved away and stumbled past Levi and Cecily into Josip's room.

The spinning stopped, and Nolia stared at the sparse furniture. There was a desk, wardrobe, and bed made of a reddish wood. The bed's black sheets were unruffled and perfectly made, and the rest of the space was neat. Not a single speck of dust out of place.

"How did you not know your husband was gone?"

"He's been avoiding her," Levi reiterated. "Likely not only because he's angry, but because he was planning *this*."

"They were living together," Nolia retorted, kneeling to check under the bed. "How could you not know?"

"I should have," Cecily said quietly. "A better wife would have known."

Nolia wasn't sure whether to wince or roll her eyes. Cecily clearly hadn't been the best spouse considering she'd stepped out of her marriage, but on the other hand, she wasn't back to her old self yet. Assuming she ever would be again after the loss of her son.

"When was the last time you saw Josip?" Nolia asked, moving to stand and ignoring Mikael's hand as he tried to assist her.

"Yesterday morning," Cecily answered. "I heard him leave his room to grab breakfast, and I quickly left my own room to try to speak to him. He went back into his room, and I couldn't convince him to come out again. Not even to eat. I begged him, promising I'd stay in my room that time, but he remained silent." Cecily's lower lip trembled. "He knows how much I despise the silent treatment, and I thought he was punishing me, but he must have already been gone."

"How?" Nolia wondered. "If he didn't leave through the front door..." Her eyes landed on the two windows that hung on either side of the bed.

"There's no windows in the washroom, so he had to escape through one of these," Mikael said, racing to the window on the right while Nolia went to the one on the left.

"These don't open," Nolia said, studying the gold panels for a lock.

"I don't see any cracks to show it was cut through," Mikael said. "Do you?"

"No," Nolia said, moving to the wall across from the one separating them from the sitting room. She knew it would be more likely to contain a secret passageway.

"You think that a servant may have helped him?" Mikael asked, following her to the wall, and starting on the opposite side of her.

They both began to tap, searching for a hollow-sounding piece of space in the stone.

"A guard helped kidnap Audrie," Nolia pointed out. "Or that's what I understood we're assuming happened."

Mikael nodded. "I've been scouring the guards all morning to see if I could find him, Your Majesty."

Instead of thanking him, Nolia found herself blurting out, "Didn't I tell you to call me by my first name?" She turned to look at him only to find that they'd searched the entirety of the wall and were now next to each other.

Mikael smiled, almost shyly. "Yes, you did. I'm sorry, *Nolia*."

Nolia's knees felt weak, and her heart was beating so loudly she wouldn't have been able to hear him if he said anything else.

"Um, guys?"

Nolia's face burned as she quickly turned to Levi, an excuse on the tip of her tongue when she saw that he wasn't looking at them. He was hovering by the desk, the papers a mess all over it. He held one in his hands.

Nolia ran to him, half snatching it away, with Mikael on her heels.

To Nolia, the so-called Queen of Icaria,

The throne upon which you sit is not yours and must be returned to its rightful owner. If King Elias is not freed and returned to us at the place where your mother's heirs resided in three days' time then our leader and his heir, Audrie Casimir, will send her army upon you. The choice is yours whether or not you will escape with your life.

"Oh my gods." Nolia nearly dropped the letter. "An attack in *Audrie's* name?"

"It isn't actually her name," Mikael noted, reading over her shoulder.

"Elias wanted to give Alaric his surname, and occasionally Alaric used it," Cecily mumbled. "It used to bother Josip, but I suppose not now."

"Last names are the least of our issues at the moment," Nolia said, shaking her head. "An army of Elias' allies are setting up to attack us if we don't free him. And they have Audrie as their hostage."

Levi shook his head. "According to them she's their—"

"They kidnapped her," Nolia interrupted. "They know whose side Audrie's on, and it certainly isn't theirs. Josip and the rest of them can pretend all they like, but we know the truth. Now we need to get her back."

"How?" Mikael asked. "We don't know where she is."

"Actually we do," Nolia responded, pointing to the letter. "Or at least where she'll be tomorrow."

"The place where your mother's heirs resided?" Levi asked with a frown. "He means Miri and her daughters, doesn't he? But I thought that Her Majesty kept their location a secret in order to stop anyone from trying to free them?"

Nolia nodded. "There was a very limited number of people who knew, but I know for certain who one of them is."

"Isiris?" Levi guessed, and Nolia gave him a grim smile.

"No, my mother's favorite brother: my Uncle Thiodore."

15

Audrie

THERE WAS AN insistent tapping on the wall by where Audrie's head rested on her bed, and it was starting to drive her insane. She assumed that it was some sort of leak between the walls, although it didn't make sense how that would be possible. It hadn't rained the past couple of days so it couldn't have been seeping in through the roof. It could have been a pipe, but Audrie wasn't certain the house had plumbing. They'd given her a chamber pot that she was supposed to tuck under her bed, but she kept right by the door in case of more guests.

After a fitful night of sleep, no one had come by yet, but Audrie knew someone would in time, if only to feed her. She stared at the tops of the trees while the sky grew brighter and brighter. The dripping continued and she counted every sound. She was nearly to a thousand when she heard footsteps in the hallway.

Finally, Audrie thought, her stomach grumbling its agreement. She listened to the footsteps, disappointed when they walked past her door.

But then hers opened.

"You?!" Audrie sat up, curling her hands into fists. As if the chain would allow her to hurt the girl the way she wanted to. "What in the gods' names are you doing here?"

"Shush," Meriah hissed, shutting the door after herself before holding up the same bowl and spoon that Calix had given her. "I'm here to feed you."

Audrie heard another door squeak open in the hallway and she waited until it had shut to speak again. "You shouldn't be here," she said. "I sent Lia to you days ago."

Meriah winced at the sound of her sister's name, and it made Audrie pause.

"Did she not arrive?" she breathed out. "I promise we didn't harm her. Nolia was—"

"Lia did arrive," Meriah interrupted. "Everything just didn't go the way I'd intended."

Meriah's slumped shoulders and downcast gaze were difficult for Audrie to miss. "What happened?" she asked.

Meriah handed her the bowl, this time filled with oatmeal. "I made a mistake," she admitted quietly. "I foolishly assumed that this hideout would be abandoned only for others to arrive shortly after me with news that His Majesty wasn't dead."

"So you're on his side again?" Audrie was too angry to accept the meal.

"I'm on the side that keeps me alive," Meriah answered. "Me and my sister."

Me and my sister. It wasn't all that difficult for Audrie to understand when she was more than willing to do anything for a girl that wasn't her sister.

Meriah shoved the bowl closer to Audrie, and she took it.

"Is Lia here?" Audrie asked.

"She's next door."

Audrie thought about the door she'd heard. "So you're both back to working for Elias like my offer never existed?"

Meriah rolled her eyes. "Stop acting as if it was something amazing and fantastic."

"I was trying to help you."

"The only person you wanted to help was yourself."

"As if Elias wants to help anyone other than himself," Audrie retorted. "I highly doubt he'll be very grateful if you're able to save him."

"I don't care to have his gratitude," Meriah snapped. "I've already told you whose side I'm on, and it isn't his. His Majesty's allies may think they can win this war, but they're kidding themselves. Once it's safe for us to leave here, we will."

Audrie frowned, forcing herself to scoop up a spoonful of oatmeal. "Darius," she said. "What have you done with him?"

"He's here." Meriah raised her eyebrows. "I'm surprised he hasn't tried speaking to you yet."

"Speaking to me?" Audrie's frown deepened. "How would he do that when we're both presumably locked in our own rooms?"

"Wow." Meriah let out a chuckle. "Maybe he doesn't like you as much as I thought. He's in the room next to yours."

Audrie swiftly glanced between each wall.

"The right one," Meriah said, motioning towards the wall the top of Audrie's bed was up against.

Audrie stared at it as if doing so would make it invisible and thus possible for her to see him. He was alive, but there was no way of knowing what condition he was in without seeing for herself. If Meriah had hurt him, she likely wouldn't admit to it.

Footsteps distracted Audrie from her thoughts, and she glanced towards the door.

"Another prisoner?" she asked.

"No," Meriah said. "It's your father."

Audrie's eyes widened. "My—?"

Her door opened again, and Josip stepped inside. He didn't look at her, nodding towards Meriah instead. It seemed to be an order as Meriah bowed, swiftly stepping away from the bed and leaving the room. When the door clicked shut behind her, Josip sat at the far edge of Audrie's bed.

"You haven't finished your breakfast," he commented.

Audrie threw her blankets off and stood. She immediately felt dizzy and grasped the post her chain was locked onto as she tried to glare at her father. "What's going on?" she asked. "What are you doing here?"

"Sit. Eat." Josip reached for the bowl she'd left haphazardly among her sheets. "You need your strength."

Audrie ignored his insistence. "Are Mother and Levi here too?"

Josip sighed. "No," he said. "We had to leave them behind, but they're safe. The princess won't harm them for your sake."

Audrie frowned. "I'm getting very tired of asking what's going on."

"Elias is alive, and will remain so until a new crown is made for Nolia," Josip responded. "We're going to break him out before that and reinstate you both on the throne."

"Reinstate?" Audrie repeated, clutching the bedpost tighter. "Neither one of us was on the throne in the first place! And why would I be...?" She trailed off, staring at her father who was carefully avoiding her gaze. Tears formed in the corner of her eyes. "You know that I'm yours," she said quietly. "So does Elias, he told me so himself. What are you doing?"

"What's right," Josip said. "I made a vow, and if my king needs me, I will do everything in my power to help him. To save him. Much like you tried to do with your best friend."

"Elias is *not* your best friend."

"No," Josip agreed, "but he is my friend. I won't allow him to die when the crown of Icaria is meant to be his."

"You're delusional," Audrie said, not caring if she got in trouble for speaking so frankly to her father. "Nolia is queen because she's meant to be. Icaria is a *queendom*."

"Things change."

"This won't."

Josip still refused to look at her. "Finish your breakfast," he said, handing the bowl to her.

"How did you arrange this?" Audrie asked, accepting it, but unable to eat. "You were locked in your room with Alexie's guards outside."

"I didn't," Josip said. "It was someone else who reached out to tell me what they'd come up with."

"Justina," Audrie said, the name leaving a sour taste in her mouth, and Josip nodded.

Audrie finally sat, nearly collapsing onto the mattress as she clutched the bowl in her two hands. None of this was her father's plan, but he was happily following it.

Josip took her silence as an invitation, and he inched closer to her. "Would it be so horrible to go along with this?" he asked. "You'd be *Queen Audrie*. You could wear pretty dresses, eat delicious food every day, and I could find you the finest man in all of Icaria to marry."

"I won't marry anyone you pick for me," Audrie said, thinking it was an odd thing for him to mention. She'd never discussed the topic of marriage with him, but she could only guess Cecily had mentioned their conversations to him. She wondered if he meant she'd undergo a Competition of Knights like Nolia. She didn't see how that would be possible, seeing as how the Tower of Icaria had been destroyed.

"What about someone you've already picked for yourself?" Josip answered. "I did my research on that boy Darius that you brought to the coronation. He has a sister that will receive his mother's title, but will likely receive a large inheritance. He also did incredibly well in the Competition, and despite what he did at the coronation—which clearly had more to do with you—he's shown himself loyal to His Majesty. He was the one who warned him about your true identity."

How did you find out all of that? was the first thing Audrie wanted to ask, but she didn't want to know why he'd thought to learn about Darius at all.

"I haven't picked him," she told her father. *And if I did, he wouldn't pick me in return*, she added to herself, but somehow he knew she was thinking it.

"You could pick him," Josip said. "He wouldn't turn down a queen."

Darius certainly wouldn't, especially with how determined he'd been to win the Competition. He'd even treated Rubin terribly in his attempt to succeed.

"Don't you see how much better your life would be if you were a princess?" Josip pushed. "If you could become queen?"

The hope in her father's voice made Audrie's stomach churn. "I wasn't meant to be either of those things, and I don't want to be," she told him. "Father, do you really know me at all if you think I'd find royal life appealing?"

"Of course it's appealing," Josip said. "Who wouldn't want to live lavishly?"

"It's not about that; it's about how I don't want to be in charge of an entire country!" Audrie exclaimed. "I don't want people looking to me to lead them when I can hardly make good decisions for myself. I'd destroy Icaria one way or another if I were queen."

"You can get all of the perks of being queen without actually ruling," Josip said. "I'll deal with the politics and—"

"So that's what this is about," Audrie interrupted, staring at her father as if she'd never seen him before. "*You* want to be king."

"No, I want to help you rule."

"By doing everything yourself? Making all the decisions that you think are best?"

"You complained—"

"Don't lie to me!" Audrie burst out. "Power is why you admitted to agreeing to Elias' coup in the first place, and it's still the reason you're willing to help him. Alaric loved you like a father, and he would have followed your advice, but he wouldn't have let you get away with ruling for him. Not like you could with me."

"Don't act as if I wouldn't make an excellent regent," Josip told her.

"Regent? I'm not a child anymore, Father," Audrie snapped. "If you put me on Icaria's throne then it's mine. I won't share it with you or a husband or anyone else. It'll be entirely *mine*."

Josip's eyes flashed angrily. "You're not going to agree to my plan, are you?"

"No," Audrie said. "I would never take something that doesn't belong to me, much less something of Nolia's."

Josip slowly shook his head before standing. "You'll change your mind in time," he said. "Once you learn to be grateful, you'll forget it was never supposed to be yours."

• • •

Audrie couldn't be certain how long had passed, but she was still tempted to scream at Josip. She wanted to tell him that his plan would never succeed. She wanted to tell him that he would only hurt himself and their family. She wanted to tell him to come back, to beg her father to be just her father for once.

Audrie grabbed the cold metal of the chain around her wrist, spinning it around to look at the lock, wondering where the key was. She wouldn't have been surprised if her father was the one who had it.

A noise came from the wall, interrupting her thoughts, much louder than the tapping had been. It was sharp and quick and Audrie was clueless as to what it possibly could be. She was about to press her ear to the wall when it stopped.

Then the point of a blade shot through the wall above her head.

Audrie jumped to her feet, watching it cut a hole in the wood. It evenly followed the sides of the planks before disappearing back through the wall. The plank of wood crashed to the floor.

"Audrie?"

Two faces stared at her through the hole.

"Oh my gods." Audrie pointed at the piece of wood. "My father is going to be furious. He's going to think I did this."

"Relax, we sliced the wood in a very particular way so that we can stick it back inside." Lia motioned for Audrie to pick it up before showing her how to do so; back in the wall, the wood didn't look as if it had been cut through at all. The only issue was getting it back out again, which Audrie needed to use her nails in order to pry out.

"Whose idea was this?" Audrie asked, setting the wood next to her on the bed in case she quickly needed to shut the hole. "And how did you learn how to do this?"

"I'm a spy. I was taught to do a variety of things like this," Lia retorted. "As for whose idea, it was Darius'. He was desperate to speak to you."

Audrie glanced at Darius, whose face was above Lia's and slightly further away since he didn't seem to want to crowd the girl as they peered through.

"I wasn't desperate," he objected, blushing.

"But you've been asking about her all—"

"No, I haven't." Darius' cheeks were redder now, and Audrie could feel her own face warming. Her heart was also fluttering, but she willed it to stop, reminding herself that Darius already had someone he cared about, and it certainly wasn't her.

"This is the second time we've ended up as prisoners together," Audrie commented. "Both times have been my fault, so I'm sure Darius wanted to complain again like last time."

Darius' lips twisted into a sneer. "That's right," he said. "This time I'm more innocent than the last, but I'll likely die here because of your stupid attempt to rehabilitate two spies. All for your best friend who probably won't be breaking you out of here."

"I'm sure she's looking for me as we speak," Audrie snapped.

"Gods above." Lia rolled her eyes. "I'm leaving now. Keep your voices down, and don't forget to put the wood back in place when you hear footsteps."

Her face disappeared from sight, Darius barely moving out of her way as she left. Audrie heard rather than saw her slam the door and stomp down the hallway.

"I think she's tired of arguments," Darius commented. "It's all she and Meri have been doing since she arrived."

Audrie knew that there were important things to focus on, but she found herself blurting out, "Meri? Since when are you so familiar with her?"

Darius frowned. "It's what Lia calls her. I didn't realize you didn't since you think they're your friends."

Audrie rolled her eyes, and Darius stepped closer to the hole to look at her.

"What happened?" he asked quietly. "How did you end up here? The sisters wouldn't tell me."

Audrie fiddled with the chain on her wrist. "One moment I was in Candicia, thinking that Nolia needed me, and the next I woke up here to a pretend guard and an incessant leak."

"A leak?"

"You haven't heard it? It was this annoying tapping sound on the wall." Audrie paused, listening for it. "It's quieted down now I guess. Maybe someone finally fixed whatever was causing it."

Darius stared at her as if she were an idiot. "Are you serious?"

"What?" Audrie frowned at him.

"It wasn't a leak," Darius said. "It was *me*."

"You?" Audrie repeated, quickly stepping back. "Why would you be tapping on the wall?"

Darius groaned. "To try to talk to you obviously. I see now that no one taught you the tapping code."

"You expect me to believe that those taps were a form of communication?"

"They were, and any intelligent well-bred person would have known that."

"I'm sorry I was busy learning more important things, *Lord* Darius," Audrie snapped, unsurprised when irritation flashed across his features. She'd learned rather early on that he didn't like to be reminded of his title. "Like how to be a decent human being that doesn't play with the emotions of others."

"What in the gods' names are you talking about?" Darius answered.

"I mean *Rubin*."

Darius pressed his lips together.

"He told me that the first thing you did when getting out of the dungeon was write to him," Audrie continued. "He said you promised to stay at Candicia as long as you could and write to him every day you were there. Then you turned around and kissed me."

Darius was silent for so long Audrie was about to scold him more for being so disrespectful to Rubin—since her pride wouldn't let her say the same for herself—but he gripped the wood, sticking his head closer to hers.

"I didn't plan to," Darius said, his voice low. "I didn't think I'd see you again after the way that rebel left you. Then we were alone in your room, and you were perfectly fine, asking me to *kill* the king, and I..."

When he trailed off, Audrie shook her head, leaning closer towards him. "None of that sounds like an excuse."

"It's not, alright?" Darius' face was a bright red. "It was a mistake, like you said. All I've done since I met you is make mistake after mistake. But I find that I want to make them, like right *now*."

Audrie suddenly realized that she could kiss Darius again if she wanted. Their faces were close enough that she could. And he wouldn't stop her; she could see on his face that he wanted her as terribly as she did him.

Audrie reached out, touching his face, and he melted under her touch. Darius' face inched closer to hers and his violet eyes that were always so cold stared at her warmly. They were like a fire that wanted to consume her, and she was tempted to let it.

Audrie shut her eyes, sighing as she slipped away from him. "We should be thinking about how to get out of here," she said. "I need to get back to Nolia... and you need to get back to Rubin. Right?"

Darius was silent for so long that she didn't think he was going to answer. He spun around out of her sight, and Audrie heard the bed squeak and the clanking of a chain.

"We do need a way out of here," Darius said. "What were you thinking?"

16

Nolia

IF NOLIA HAD known that being queen meant that she'd be locked in her room often, she didn't know if she would have been so interested in the position. Isiris and Alexie went on and on about how it was for her own safety, and her council agreed. She'd been tempted to veto their vote that she remain at Candicia, but her Uncle Thiodore had begged her to stay. She didn't know how much of it had to do with his wanting to keep her safe and his desire to keep her away from the place Miri and her daughters had been imprisoned for so many years.

Nolia decided she'd burn down the building once Audrie had been rescued.

"You're not going to be able to see anything from here," Nolia commented as Yadira paused by one of the tea room's windows for the hundredth time. She was the only lady she hadn't sent away because Yadira had insisted on staying.

"That depends on what she's looking for," Giana commented, hovering out of Nolia's sight to the side of the couch.

"The Alders, I'm presuming," Nolia replied, hoping her tone didn't sound as grouchy to everyone else as it did to herself.

"Cilia's surname is Kimura," Yadira told her, grabbing one of the curtains as she almost pressed her nose to the glass. "She said she'd come say goodbye before she and Mikael leave."

"At least you've won over one of your in-laws." Nolia sighed, staring at Katrine's book in her lap. She'd grabbed it yet again with the intention of reading, but she couldn't possibly bring her mind to focus.

Giana let out a choked laugh. "I'd say Isiris likes you as much as she possibly can."

"I agree." Yadira glanced back at Nolia, a hint of envy in her dark eyes. "Who wouldn't love having you as a daughter-in-law? Whoever you marry gets to be king."

It's a rather shallow reason for loving me though, isn't it? Nolia thought, but she only nodded with a tense smile. She'd had her entire life to get used to being seen as a prize, and yet it made her skin crawl.

A guard appeared then to announce Isidore's arrival, and Nolia stood, setting the book to the side while she smoothed down her skirt, preparing to greet him. She hated that she'd been hoping it was Mikael, and tried to remind herself that he only would be stopping by to see Yadira before he left to help rescue Audrie.

"Don't you find it odd that despite being your fiancé, Isidore still has to be allowed permission into your room?" Yadira commented.

A flurry of responses came to mind as Nolia opened her mouth, but no words escaped her lips. One voice wanted to remind her that they weren't married yet, so there were different protocols; another wanted to point out that Elias had always required permission to be near his wife; and the last voice—that was definitely Corinne's—wanted to scold Yadira for making such a comment.

"It's simply the way it is for queens and almost-kings," Nolia finally said. "Some nobles too, I think."

Yadira shrugged before shaking her head. "That sort of thing isn't for me."

When Isidore appeared, Nolia was only half surprised to see Katiana in his arms. She'd requested that the baby be brought to her while they waited to hear that Audrie had been rescued. In case of an attack on the palace, she'd wanted Katiana with her so all of their best guards could be in one place.

"Thank you," Nolia told the guard who'd brought them in. "When Mikael Alder and Cilia Kimura arrive—"

Yadira grinned happily. "I can go wait for them by the door, Your Majesty. That way the guard won't have to bother you again."

Nolia almost rolled her eyes. "I suppose you may."

Yadira all but skipped out of the room, barely curtsying to Isidore, who hadn't moved from the doorway.

"Your heir, Your Majesty."

Isidore offered her the tiny bundle, and Nolia hesitated to take it. She'd hardly known how to hold her before, and this time, to her horror, the baby was awake.

"Your Majesty?" Isidore tried again, looking as uncomfortable as Nolia felt.

Nolia sat and motioned for him to hand her the child.

"Prince Kristopher was grateful you wanted to protect his daughter," Isidore said, swiftly sitting next to her to hand the baby off. His movements were gentle and careful, but he looked glad to be rid of her. "Princess Ophelia, however... she very desperately wanted to bring Katiana to you herself. I wasn't certain if you'd be alright with it, so I had to convince her to let the baby go."

Nolia couldn't help but wrinkle her nose at her uncle's new wife being referred to as a princess. Even if it was technically her title now, it didn't feel quite right. She wondered if her cousins felt the same way, especially when it was their mother Ophelia was replacing.

"She's only concerned for her child as any good parent would be," Nolia said, and Isidore nodded his agreement.

An awkward silence fell between them, and Nolia could feel the eyes of the guards watching them, their questions almost palpable in the air. *What kind of parents will they make? Will they pay them any attention or leave them to their governess? Will they get along for the sake of their children better than Katrine and Elias did?*

Nolia stared at Katiana, her body squirming its way out of the dark purple blanket she'd arrived in. She wore nothing but a diaper underneath, so Nolia tried to cover her in case she found the air too cold. But Katiana didn't seem to mind, yawning as she lifted her arms over her head.

Isidore scooted the tiniest bit closer to Nolia as he tried to help her cover the baby. "Perhaps I should have asked for a larger blanket," he said. "It didn't look quite so small before..."

"It's alright, it isn't as if I haven't got plenty here," Nolia replied.

"Yes, but this is a baby blanket." Isidore tried to get Katiana's feet back into the blanket while Nolia tried to wrap the blanket over her stomach.

"I sincerely doubt there's a difference," she said.

Isidore frowned. "Of course there is."

"What's the difference?"

"I... don't know."

Giana stepped closer. "Um, Your Majesties, you may want to be more—"

Katiana let out a wail, and Nolia almost jumped.

"Gentle." Giana winced.

"Oh my gods," Nolia mumbled. "What did we do? Is she hurt?"

"No, she's hungry."

Nolia's head swung around to see that Yadira had led Mikael and Cilia inside, and she almost cursed. The audience watching her terrible attempt at parenting was growing apparently.

"How would you know?" Isidore asked, his hands hovering over Katiana's small writhing body. She'd flung the blanket completely off, and he appeared unsure of whether or not to try covering her again.

"I have four younger sisters," Mikael replied. "Three of which I helped care for as babies."

"He always knew what they wanted," Cilia agreed. "He can tell the difference between their cries."

"I don't have milk," Nolia said, trying not to panic. "Isn't that all she can eat?"

"Your aunt didn't send you a bottle?" Mikael looked alarmed now. "Or diapers or—?"

"There." Isidore pointed to one of the guards that was holding a large leather bag. "She threw quite a bit of things inside."

Giana reached to grab it, but Mikael got to the guard first. His tranquility had returned as he rifled through the items before he found a bottle already filled with milk.

"This one's warm, but you may want to send the others to the kitchen for when she gets hungry again later," he commented.

I'll have to feed her again? Nolia almost blurted out. Instead she waved Mikael over to her wildly. But when he offered her the bottle, Nolia paused, realizing that while she thought she may know how to feed Katiana, she couldn't be certain. What if she drowned her tiny lungs in milk?

"Here, let me help you." Mikael kneeled before Nolia, placing a hand over the arm supporting Katiana's head and another over Nolia's, showing her the angle to hold the bottle at.

"This isn't too difficult," Nolia said, unable to stop herself from grinning as Katiana drank hungrily.

"That's because you're a natural." Mikael gazed at her. "You'll make a wonderful mother someday, Nolia."

And you'll be a great father, Nolia wanted to say, but the moment the thought came to mind, her eyes drifted back to Yadira. She was beaming at something Cilia had said and was whispering into her ear.

"I think that it's time we take our leave, *Your Majesty*."

Nolia glanced over at Isidore, who was frowning.

"Come on, Mikael," he said as he stood. "*Her Majesty* should be able to manage on her own now. Thanks to your assistance."

Mikael glanced from Katiana to Nolia. "I suppose it's getting late. If you have any other issues, I'm sure someone else here knows about babies."

"Yadira perhaps?" Isidore suggested, making the girl quickly glance up from Cilia.

Nolia was about to tell him that Yadira would know less considering she was the youngest of her family when Mikael cleared his throat.

"Yes, Yadira," he said as if he'd forgotten about her.

Guilt hit Nolia like a slap. "I'm sorry, Mikael. You should have been spending this time with Yadira instead of trying to teach me basic maternal skills," she said. "You came to say goodbye to her, after all."

"I didn't." Mikael cleared his throat again before adding, "I mean not only her. I wanted to see you before I left—to reassure you I'll do everything I can to return Audrie to you."

Nolia nodded. "I know you will, just..." She trailed off, unsure how to continue.

"Nolia?" Mikael asked.

"Come back too?" Nolia said, keeping her voice low.

Mikael's eyes were bright as he squeezed her arm holding Katiana.

"Mikael," Isidore said, already standing. "We should leave *Her Majesty* now."

It took Nolia a moment to realize why Isidore was making so much of an emphasis on her title. He'd heard Mikael call her by her first name. And from the look on his face, he wasn't pleased.

Mikael's fingers slipped away from her, and he went to his sister and Yadira. Nolia didn't watch him go; the last thing she needed was to see the tearful farewell Yadira would give Mikael.

Instead, Nolia stood to grab Isidore's arm before he could step away from her. He tensed under her touch, but she tried to smile.

"You're my fiancé," she told him quietly. "I'd very much like it if you came back safely as well."

Isidore stared at her for a moment, relaxing before he nodded. "I never thought differently, Your Majesty, but it's nice to hear," he said. "I'll assure you I don't have any intention of dying or letting those you love die either. I'll bring everyone back to you." His eyes drifted to the doorway where Mikael and Cilia were waiting for him. "I promise."

• • •

It turned out that Giana was rather good with babies. That or Katiana hated Nolia, which the teenage queen was choosing to believe wasn't the case.

She'd fallen asleep in the guard's arms, and everyone had been too afraid to move her in case she awoke screaming her newborn wails. They weren't all that loud, but Nolia hated hearing them, especially since she couldn't tell what the cries meant like Mikael.

"How long are they supposed to be gone for?" Yadira asked, having barely moved from her spot by the window.

"If I knew, I'd be much less anxious," Nolia replied, her fingers trembling as she tried to embroider her initials into a handkerchief for Isidore.

It's time you get to know your fiancé, to really *know him*, Nolia was trying to convince herself. If they were going to be spending the rest of their lives together and having children, they needed to get along better than her parents had.

"Alexie or Isiris didn't give you an estimate?"

Nolia nearly pricked herself and quickly set the handkerchief down in her lap. "No, there's no way of receiving an estimate when you don't know what you're walking into," she said.

"Aren't you supposed to scout the area beforehand?" Yadira asked with a frown.

"That isn't possible with war," Giana answered for Nolia. She shifted her weight between her feet, gently rocking Katiana.

Nolia watched, trying to focus on the sweetness of what she saw as opposed to what she'd heard.

So long as the people of Icaria are flourishing and at peace, so will the rest of the world be, Candice had warned the Icarians when she'd established the queendom. Now they were no longer flourishing or at peace. What would that mean for their world?

Giana suddenly stopped rocking Katiana, standing up straight as she clutched the baby to herself tighter with a frown. "Did you hear that?"

Nolia stiffened, dropping her embroidery altogether. "Hear what?"

Giana pressed one finger to her lips, and the room fell into silence, everyone straining their ears to listen.

A minute passed before Giana shook her head. "Must not have been any—"

A scream rang out, making Nolia's blood run cold.

"Gods," Yadira whimpered.

"Secure the room!" Giana called out, rushing to hand Nolia the baby while the guards raced around. Yadira was dragged away from the window to Nolia where they swiftly hustled to the wall across from the tea room's entrance, where the servants' doorway was.

"What's—?" Yadira began, but Giana silenced her with a hand.

"If the rebels break into the room, go through the passageway," she ordered.

"There's a passageway here?" Nolia wasn't able to stop herself from bursting out. "Why does no one ever think it important to tell me about escape related things?"

"Perhaps because the last time you escaped, you weren't supposed to?" When Nolia glared at Yadira, she offered a lame curtsy. "Your Majesty?"

"We don't have time to argue," Giana snapped. "If they get into the room, just *go*. Promise me you will."

Nolia hesitated before nodding. It wasn't only her life possibly in danger, it was Katiana's too, and she was nothing but an innocent baby. *Why did you have to insist on keeping her with you?* Nolia scolded herself. She was beginning to think she would have been safer if she'd stayed with her family.

The guards spread out around them while others remained by the windows and the room's entrance.

Please, gods, Nolia prayed, clutching the newborn closer to her chest. The commotion had woken Katiana, but she wasn't crying, only staring up curiously at what was around her.

Nolia was too afraid to think of any single god to pray to, her mind swirling with all the possibilities. Cadoc, the god of war, to help them win? Or Nuncio, the god of prophecy and fortune, to bring them luck? Or Azrail, the god of the afterlife, to lead the souls they would lose in battle to the gods' realm? Or Irina, the goddess of peace, to—

Mirah. The thought hit Nolia so hard it almost knocked her into the wall. She didn't know why her mind called out to Mirah, why her soul had always felt linked to the goddess of the sea and water. Especially when her queendom had tried to conquer Icaria years before, and especially *now* when there wasn't anything Mirah could possibly do to keep them safe. But still, Nolia prayed.

"Mirah, great goddess, I beg you to hear me," she whispered, shutting her eyes tightly. "Please bring us out of this alive and well."

Nolia began to repeat her plea over and over again, and eventually she heard Yadira's voice join hers. They huddled together, backs pressed against the wall, waiting for what would happen next.

The door to the queen's apartment was ripped off its hinges.

Nolia would have screamed if Yadira hadn't first, and Giana turned to Nolia, her eyes reminding her of her promise.

Nolia scrambled to find a way to open the passageway while Yadira stood by her, frozen with fear. She could see the prayer they'd been in the middle of on the tip of her tongue, and she swiftly kicked Yadira's shin.

"Help me!" she hissed.

Yadira jumped to search the wall, but she didn't have any better luck.

Shouts and the clang of swordplay thundered behind Nolia, the swoosh of arrows flying and bodies falling. It was coming closer as the rebels made their way down the hallway.

"There's nothing here," Yadira wailed. "We're going to die and I'm never going to be able to tell Cilia that—!"

Nolia's fingers pressed into a piece of the paneling and it sank into the wall, causing an incredibly well disguised door to swing backward.

"You're a genius!" Yadira looked as if she would have jumped into Nolia's arms if Katiana hadn't already been there.

"Go!" Giana shouted at them. "And don't look—*no!*" Her eyes widened as she stared at the open wall.

Nolia scrambled away as rebels poured out of the passageway.

"How did they know?" Yadira shrieked as a rebel grabbed her.

Giana positioned herself in front of Nolia while another guard stood at her back.

"His Majesty was very detailed in his descriptions of the palace when he was attempting to recruit me."

Nolia's knees nearly gave out underneath her. "Justina?"

The rebel stepped into the light, smiling as if she'd dropped by for tea.

How did you get out of your room? was the first question that came to mind, but it was swiftly followed by others. *How did you get your rebels inside? Was your deal ever genuine? Why did you allow yourself to be captured?*

"I hope you don't mind," Justina said, shrugging. "I heard the commotion and decided I'd help."

"You're helping?" Nolia repeated as Giana snorted, her sword pointed at the woman.

"Of course," Justina replied, her smile unwavering. "I'm here to bring you to safety. Hence, the use of this passageway. Now come along."

"She's not going anywhere with you," Giana answered. "Now how about you get out of here while you can?"

Justina pressed a hand to her lips as if surprised, but Nolia could see the smirk she was trying to hide.

"You can stop pretending now," Nolia snapped. "You're nothing but a liar, aren't you? You've been working for my father all along."

Justina laughed. "I've lied about many things, but not about that."

If Nolia had been holding anything other than a baby, she would have thrown it at Justina.

"As if the technicalities matter," she said. "The point is that you're here to kill me so he can take the throne."

"Certainly not." Justina unsheathed the sword hanging on her hip. "I'm here to kill you so my niece can."

17

Audrie

THERE WAS NO plan. Audrie and Darius had stayed up all night talking, but they hadn't come up with anything. He'd taught her the basics of the tapping code, and she'd explained her suspicions about Justina and the sisters, but there was no plan.

They were stuck.

They had no entertainment except for each other, and Meriah and Lia when they came to feed them. But they weren't interested in telling Audrie or Darius anything useful. Meriah had made it incredibly clear that they wouldn't risk helping them escape either.

Now Audrie and Darius had run out of things to talk about, and she was still refusing to resort to other things, even with the stares Darius gave her. If they'd been in the same room, they likely wouldn't have been able to help themselves.

"Do you think Nolia has sent out a search party for you yet?"

Audrie lay flat on her bed, staring at her ceiling. Darius had given up staring at her through the wall, and she wondered if he was in a similar position.

"Yes," Audrie said. "It won't be anything as intense as it was when she was missing though."

"She must not love you all that much then."

Audrie glared at the wall. "I'm her commoner best friend, I'm not as important as the *crown princess*."

"I suppose it depends who you ask whether or not you're as important," Darius said thoughtfully. "Since some people like your father think you're His Majesty's heir."

Audrie rolled her eyes. "Those people are idiots."

"My mother would be incredibly displeased with me if I called her an idiot."

Audrie raised her head slightly, glancing at the hole in the wall. "I was beginning to think you didn't have a family," she said carefully. "You've never mentioned them, you never wanted to write to them..."

Darius let out a bitter laugh. "I'd have to have a family in order to be a lord like you like to remind me I am."

"I can't say it makes sense to me why that bothers you so much either." Audrie rolled to her side to prop herself up on her elbow.

"I don't know why you care."

Audrie flipped onto her back, taking satisfaction in the bed squeaking loudly. "I don't know either," she snapped. "You sure do make it impossible to like you most of the time."

Darius didn't respond, and after a moment of silence, Audrie stood to get the plank of wood. "Supper is probably coming soon, so we should—"

"Being a lord doesn't mean anything when it's an empty title."

Audrie paused, the wood gripped in her hands as she peered through the hole. Darius wasn't on his bed, instead sitting on the ground by it.

"I'm my mother's first child," Darius continued, "but I'm never going to inherit anything because I'm a boy. There's enough for my twin sister and me to share, but she'll get everything, like she has our whole lives."

Darius looked up, his violet eyes the most vulnerable Audrie had ever seen them. It made her want to kiss him again more than ever.

Before Audrie could come up with some sort of response, footsteps echoed through the hallway outside their doors. Footsteps that were much louder than that of Meriah's or Lia's.

Audrie shoved the plank of wood into place as her door opened.

"Father." Audrie was tempted to whip around to face him, but she didn't know if it would be more suspicious of her to continue staring at the wall or let him see the panic in her eyes. So she crossed her arms and kept her back to him as if she were being stubborn.

"Audrie." Josip sighed, clearly buying it. When Audrie didn't move, he came to sit at the edge of her bed. "I wanted to see you before I left."

Audrie wasn't able to stop herself from glancing at him. "Where are you going?"

"To free His Majesty."

Audrie's hands curled into fists, and she turned to face him. "Don't be stupid," she told him. "You're going to risk your life for —"

"I'm not here to argue this matter with you," Josip interrupted. "I'm here to say goodbye." He hesitated before adding, "To tell you that I love you, Audrie, that everything I'm doing is for your benefit."

Audrie shook her head. "Stop insisting that this isn't for you. You're putting my life and Mother's and Levi's all in danger because *you* want to be king. You're so obsessed with power that you're willing to work with someone you don't trust."

Josip frowned. "Elias and I—"

"I mean Justina."

"She *volunteered* to help us free His Majesty; it doesn't matter to me what she wants."

Josip was staring at her firmly, but as his daughter, Audrie knew better. He was more concerned than she was about what Justina would ask for once the rebellion was over. She was certainly the type to not care if they won either; she'd demand her reward either way.

"You'll be safe here until I return for you." Josip stood up as suddenly as he'd sat down. "The attack should be rather quick since we outnumber the remaining palace guards by a considerable amount."

Audrie gave him a look. "Remaining? What did you do?"

"You think so lowly of me now, don't you?" Josip rolled his eyes. "We've simply created a diversion elsewhere for the royal armies to focus on. No need to worry about it."

"Tell me," Audrie insisted, crossing her arms again. "It isn't as if I can tell anyone."

Josip smiled wistfully. "Not when I trust you so little."

The words stung more than Audrie wished they had. She blinked quickly to keep her tears at bay. Josip had never had the patience for her tears when she was a child, and he certainly wouldn't now as a young woman. Especially when he wanted her to be the strong queen to replace Nolia. Nolia, who already was the strongest person Audrie knew.

"Father, please," Audrie whispered. "Don't do this. They'll kill you, they'll kill me, they'll kill—"

Josip reached out to touch her arm. "You'll be safe so long as you remain here, Audrie. Our people have been carefully instructed to guard you from any possible dangers, and your mother and brother will also be taken care of once we get to them."

Audrie wanted to ask how he could be so certain about everything when he didn't trust Justina. How could he put the fate of his family in the hands of someone who didn't want the same thing as him?

"Father—"

"Hush, Audrie." Josip touched her cheek for a moment before his hand slipped away. "Sleep. By the time you wake, everything will be over."

Audrie watched him step towards the door, and her mind raced with ways to stop him, to think of any sort of plan that she and

Darius hadn't been able to come up with. But there wasn't anything. She was nothing but a little girl begging her father to listen to her.

But maybe that was all she needed to be.

"Father, if you do this, I'll never forgive you."

Josip paused, his fingers on the doorknob. "You will," he said after a moment. "Someday."

"I won't," Audrie promised, stepping as close to him as the chain on her wrist allowed. "And when you get caught, I won't intercede with Nolia on your behalf. I'll arrange your execution myself."

Josip smiled, and she could tell he didn't believe her. "I'll see you soon."

• • •

Audrie didn't have the time to unlatch the plank of wood from the wall before rebels appeared to kill her.

At first, she thought that she was being paranoid, since what reason would they have to murder the supposed heir of their leader? Josip had also already said that they were there to protect her. Then she realized that one of her so-called protectors was incredibly familiar.

"You." Audrie's eyes widened as she recognized him.

He grinned at her, the same way he had when he'd freed her from Candicia's dungeon before trying to squish her insides out through her sword wound.

"Intelligent little thing," he said. "I'd wondered whether or not you would remember me."

You don't forget your would-be murderer, Audrie almost told him. Instead she began tapping on the wall, one of the few codes Darius had taught her: *help*.

"Don't you dare come near me," Audrie hissed, her back pressed against the wall as her fingers finished relaying the message. She looked from him to the other rebel who had entered with him, smiling just as maliciously.

"We don't need to be close to kill you," he said. "Do we, Ursila?"

"Not when I have such good aim," Ursila agreed, holding up her dagger. "Isn't that right, Orion?"

"I'm your *princess*," Audrie tried, wanting to tap again, but afraid that they would notice. Or worse, know that she was calling for help.

The rebels laughed, the one who'd already tried to kill her loudest of all.

"You aren't anyone's princess," Orion told her.

Ursila crept forward, and Orion swung his arm out to stop her. "She got away once," he said. "I won't let it happen again."

The rebel pounced at her, but Audrie managed to move out of his grasp, so he slammed into the wall instead. She quickly kicked him, not very hard since she was at an awkward angle being squished between him and the bed before Ursila was racing towards her.

"She's mine!" Orion howled, but she didn't listen.

Audrie jumped onto her bed, and Ursila followed.

"Your life is mine," she said, raising the dagger over her head.

Audrie shrank back, knowing that the wall trick wouldn't work nearly as well when her opponent had an incredibly sharp object in her hands, but tried dodging again.

The move only worked because the chain got in the way. The dagger connected with the metal, creating a loud clang that made Audrie's head vibrate, but did nothing to harm the chain. It didn't even look dented.

"Are you trying to free her?" Orion snapped.

"No, I—"

Ursila dropped the dagger as he grabbed her hair and dragged her off the bed.

"My dagger, you imbecile!" Ursila exclaimed as Audrie dove for it.

"You'll get it back," Orion replied, shoving Ursila onto the floor across from him. "It isn't as if she can do anything with it against us."

A possibly stupid idea came to mind, and Audrie clutched the dagger tighter. The smart thing would be to hold onto her only weapon, but he was right. What good would a dagger do against the two swords at the rebels' sides?

Audrie threw the dagger straight at Orion's head. Ursila cried out, and he turned in time for the small blade to slice through his forehead.

Audrie screamed too as his body fell, and she launched herself from the bed, falling hard on her knees to grab the sword at his side.

Ursila's lips twisted into a snarl, but before she could speak, the door flew open, and Lia stepped inside.

She calmly glanced at the body on the floor. "I suppose I should have only brought dinner for two?"

Ursila bolted, shoving Lia out of her way as she scrambled out of the room.

"Why leave?" Lia called out. "His Majesty will find you wherever you end up!"

Audrie loosened her grip on the sword. "You have quite the timing," she said. "Especially since you're clearly not here to feed me."

Lia wriggled her empty fingers in agreement. "The house had already been cleared out, and Meri and I were leaving until I heard Darius shouting for us."

Darius was shouting? Audrie went over her memory of the past few minutes, searching for the sound of his voice. But she didn't think she'd heard him once.

Audrie motioned towards the chain. "Do you happen to have the key for this thing?"

Lia smiled. "No."

"I do."

Meriah appeared behind Lia, a ring of keys in one hand and a pale wrist in her other. She dragged Darius into the room after her, giving him a pointed look that said *stay* before she let go of him to unchain Audrie.

"Thank the gods," Audrie breathed out, not caring that Meriah was being incredibly ungentle with her hand as she shoved the key into the lock. "What changed your mind about helping us?"

"I didn't," Meriah replied, giving her sister a look that made it obvious to Audrie that Lia was the one she should be thanking. Which was a surprise when Lia had originally been the one against helping them.

"We had no idea they planned to kill you," Lia said as the lock popped open. "We wouldn't have let them in otherwise."

Audrie quickly tore her wrist away from Meriah's grasp, and she would have rubbed the irritated skin with her other hand if she hadn't been still holding the sword.

Did my father know? she wondered, and immediately wished she could take the thought back. Despite everything Josip had already done, he'd never hurt her. Her father would never do something like that to her... would he?

Darius cleared his throat loudly, interrupting her spiraling mind. "Not that it isn't reassuring to hear you played no part in a murder attempt, but we need to go now," he said. "This is quite literally the moment we've been waiting for to escape."

"You're right," Audrie said. "Maybe we didn't need a plan, after all."

$$\bullet \bullet \bullet$$

The group crept down the stairs, careful in case the house wasn't empty. Meriah claimed that she'd checked that it was to be certain no one would catch her and Lia deserting the house, but she clearly wasn't convinced. No one else was either, so they held their breaths until they made it to the front door.

"Stay here," Meriah said, her hand on the doorknob and the other on the sword at her belt. Two daggers had also been strapped to her back, and Audrie wondered if they were meant for Lia since, as far as she could see, the girl was weaponless.

"We can help," Audrie insisted.

"You'll only get us caught," Meriah responded. "We'll come get you once we have the horses."

She opened the door, and she and Lia sprinted out of the house.

"We should have asked where we were," Audrie mumbled, watching them through the window. Now that she could see the front of the house, she realized that it wasn't all that different from what she'd seen in her bedroom window. All that was visible to them was trees.

Darius grimaced as he wiped the dagger they'd pulled out of Orion's head on the curtain next to him. "We're by where Miri and her daughters were kept imprisoned. This is the house the off-duty guards stayed in."

Audrie blinked. "How do you know that?"

"Meri told me." Darius rubbed the dagger with another piece of the curtain. "When we were on our way here."

"Why didn't you tell me that earlier?"

"You didn't ask."

Audrie scowled. "Do you know how to get back to Candicia?"

"Of course." The dagger was now clean enough to his liking, and Darius tucked it into his belt. "I think it took about an hour on horseback to get here?"

"Thank the gods." Audrie reached for the door.

Darius stopped her. "We're supposed to wait."

"We don't have the time," Audrie said. "I need to go to Nolia now. My father said they set up some sort of distraction to keep the royal army away from the palace where I know she'll be." She swallowed, forcing herself to add, "Rubin is there too, also unknowingly in danger."

Darius ran a hand down his face. "I wish you'd stop bringing him up."

"I'm sorry it makes you so uncomfortable to talk about your boyfriend."

They stepped out of the house, and Darius led them in the same direction Meriah and Lia had gone.

"I don't know how it doesn't make you uncomfortable," Darius mumbled as they entered the trees.

"It does," Audrie said, accepting his hand to get over a particularly tall root in the ground. "But if *you* can't remember that you've already given yourself to someone else then I have to."

Darius appeared stung by her words, but he remained quiet as they continued further into the forest. Audrie's worries turned towards how much distance they could travel before the sun set; soon they wouldn't be able to see anything.

Her thoughts were interrupted by the ringing of metal.

Darius grabbed her arm, likely about to tell her that they should switch directions, but she shrugged him off, running towards the sound.

She stopped at the edge of where the fighting was happening, spotting Meriah defending a particularly vicious blow from Ursila. A couple of feet away was Lia attempting to fight off three other rebels. The only reason she was succeeding was because she was on a horse.

Audrie didn't have the time to question why they were fighting at all before she sprinted to help Lia.

She stabbed one of the rebels, trying not to cringe as she ripped the sword out to attack another.

"Audrie?" Lia blurted out.

"You freed her?" Ursila exclaimed. "So you're not only deserters, you're—"

Ursila began to choke, and Audrie only had a moment to glance towards her before she was blocking a jab from her opponent. A dagger was sticking out of Ursila's throat, and she had a fairly good idea who had thrown it.

"The gods must hate me," Darius was saying as he went to retrieve the weapon. "All I wanted was to be king, to live a good life, and now—"

"Enough complaining," Meriah snapped as she ran at the remaining rebel.

Darius scooped up the fallen rebel's sword to join her. It wasn't very long until the two rebels were dead too.

Audrie let out a breath of relief. "I sincerely hope that after today I never have to kill anyone again."

Darius snorted, and both sisters looked as if they wanted to say something, but the pounding of feet and voices stopped them.

"The signal came from around here!" someone shouted.

Signal? Audrie wondered as Meriah cursed.

She pointed at the two horses that had been tied to a tree before scrambling to untie one. "Get on!" she told Audrie and Darius.

Darius quickly did as she'd ordered, untangling the knot as he glared at Audrie to obey. Any other time, she likely wouldn't have listened to him, but Audrie couldn't have gotten onto the horse any quicker.

"They're here!" a voice yelled, and a flurry of arrows was shot in their direction.

Lia screamed, Meriah yelled at them to go, and Audrie barely had the time to pull Darius up behind her before they took off.

She followed Meriah, who looked back only to check that Lia was behind them. Audrie kept her head down and found some peace of mind in knowing that Darius would likely block any arrows coming toward her anyway.

Audrie didn't know how long they rode before the arrows stopped flying and the pound of hooves and voices disappeared. But Meriah didn't stop or slow her pace until they reached an ancient looking tree.

"Why are we stopping?" Audrie asked, leaning back against Darius as she tried to catch her breath.

"We have to separate," Meriah said as she prompted Lia to bring her horse to her side.

"Why can't we go with them?" Lia's chest was heaving as she waved a hand around. "They discovered us helping them, that's all the more reason—"

"None of you will be leaving."

They turned towards where the voice had come from, the figure hardly visible by the trunk in the tree's shade, and Audrie nearly fell out of her saddle.

"Oh my gods," she said. "Who would have thought I'd ever be happy to see *you*?"

18

Nolia

IT HADN'T TAKEN Nolia as long as she would have thought to find out what it was Justina wanted. The rebel had offered up the information herself. Not that it made any sense.

Your niece? Who's your niece? Nolia wanted to ask. She would have if Justina hadn't pointed a sword at her.

"Remember, Nolia remains unharmed," Justina said. "She doesn't die until I say she does."

The fighting in the room had never ceased, but now the rebels who had come with Justina sprang into action too.

"Stay behind me, Your Majesty," Giana said, her teeth gritted as a rebel flew towards her.

The women locked in battle, and Nolia could hear that the guard behind her was also busy fighting off rebels. She itched to grab a weapon herself, to fight in the battle they were obviously outnumbered in. But even if she found a sword, who would take care of Katiana?

Yadira. Nolia quickly looked for her lady-in-waiting. She hadn't received any type of battle training, so she wouldn't be part of the fight. If she could get Katiana to her, she could hold the baby while Nolia helped.

Once she spotted Yadira, Nolia quickly realized why that would be a bad idea. Yadira was kicking and scratching the guard who'd grabbed her, clearly knowing that she wouldn't win, but trying anyway. Yadira's lack of training made it so that she couldn't protect herself, much less a newborn.

The rebel slapped Yadira so hard that she fell to the ground, and Nolia cried out.

The sound caught Giana's attention, likely thinking that Nolia had been harmed, and it gave her opponent the upper hand. She swung her sword so quickly that Giana didn't have the chance to defend herself. The blade pierced Giana's stomach.

Nolia screamed again as her guard fell, and she could see out of the corner of her eye that Yadira's rebel was reaching for his sword.

"Stop!" Nolia shrieked. "Everyone please—!"

"No more lives will be lost if you come with me."

Nolia didn't realize that she'd collapsed to her knees until she was staring at Justina's brown boots, only a few inches away from Giana's body. She didn't dare set Katiana down, keeping the wailing baby in her arms as she tore off pieces of her gown to press onto Giana, who wasn't conscious enough to stop the bleeding herself. The gentle duck egg shade quickly stained red.

Nolia's stomach twisted as her palms became wet with blood. The feeling grew worse when she spotted Yadira's rebel with blood on his blade. "Order them to stand down," she said. "Prove you'll keep your word."

"I swear on the gods." Justina smiled. "On Mirah, specifically."

Nolia ripped off the largest piece of her gown she could before pressing it to Giana's wound. The guard's eyes fluttered. "Nolia?" she choked out, but Nolia shushed her.

"You're going to be alright," she told her, praying that she wasn't lying. "Just hold on."

• • •

Nolia gagged the moment they left the queen's apartment. The battle in the tea room had been terrible, but there hadn't been nearly as much bloodshed as there was in the hallway outside her rooms.

"It's admirable how much your servants love you," Justina commented. "So many, so willing to give their lives to protect you."

Nolia didn't answer, clutching Katiana closer as she followed Justina, guilty that she was too afraid to look at the bodies of her guards. At first, she told herself that the rebels surrounding her were in the way, but they began to trickle away until eventually there were only two behind her.

"Where are your rebels going?" Nolia asked. "You swore they would leave my people alone."

"I swore we would leave your household alone," Justina replied. "There are other people in Candicia that need to be taken care of."

"No, there isn't," Nolia swiftly lied. There were nobles who had decided to stay, and her Uncle Kristopher and his family. But why would Justina care about them when she already had Nolia?

And Katiana, Nolia remembered, staring down at the infant.

Justina laughed. "You're a terrible liar."

"You think you're a better one?" Nolia answered. "Everyone knew you weren't here to offer an alliance."

"Yet you allowed me to stay, didn't you?"

Justina paused, glancing between hallways before she took one to their right.

Nolia frowned, confused herself as to where Justina thought they were going. "It's better to have you here than wandering out in Icaria," she said. "So how did you manage to use that to your advantage? Since clearly, you *wanted* to be locked away."

"Wouldn't you like to know."

Nolia realized then that there were a lot of things she was curious about regarding Justina. If she played her cards right, maybe the rebel would tell her. Perhaps she could distract her enough to escape.

The odds weren't in her favor, but the very least she could do for herself was try.

"I would," Nolia said. "You've fascinated me for as long as I can remember. You were the only rebel that I ever thought may genuinely want what's best for Icaria." Justina didn't look at her, but Nolia could tell she was flattered. "You were eager to work with my mother, despite all those times she tried to trap you," she pushed. "Why? Was it all for show?"

"Not necessarily," Justina replied after a moment. "It simply would have been easier if she'd thought of me as an ally before I struck. A house falls more easily if its base is weak; your father had a similar mindset."

"So you had the same plan?"

"Not quite."

"Right," Nolia mumbled. "Elias wants to put himself on the throne, and you want to put your niece."

Justina glanced back at her. "Would you willingly give up your throne?" she asked. "Would you support a different queen if it were rightfully hers?"

Nolia frowned again. "Who's your niece?"

Justina looked away, pausing again as if finding the hallway unfamiliar. Nolia knew exactly where they were, nearing Elias' old room. Which she realized she would likely have to move Isidore into soon, even if he wasn't king yet. Nolia had no idea where he was staying—not that it was something she *wanted* to know.

Nolia quickly reminded herself of the things she did.

"All these years, has this always been about her?" Nolia asked before Justina could move again. "It hasn't been about taxes or famine or any of the other things you've complained about?"

"Of course," Justina said. "Those were issues that could be dealt with once she was on the throne. Not that there would be very many rebels left, seeing as how your father and I have been the leaders of most of them."

Justina seemed to decide they were in the right place before she continued down a hallway.

"Why your niece?" Nolia hurried after her. "Why not yourself?"

"The throne is not mine," Justina said. "It's hers. I'd keep her seat warm while we waited for her to appear, but that would be all."

So she isn't in Icaria, Nolia thought, her confusion growing. Where could she be? The mainland was the most obvious answer, but they weren't as welcoming to immigrants like Icaria was. The mainland countries expected their people to remain within the place of their birth to worship the god they'd been born under.

"We must be distant cousins or something," Nolia commented. "From a different line of the Rionas?"

Justina laughed. "She's *not* a Riona. She's something much greater."

They passed the entrance of the king's room, and stopped further down the hall in front of a portrait of Elias and Katrine on their wedding day. Nolia couldn't help but grimace at her parents' unhappy stares.

So why get married? Nolia wished she could ask her mother. The Katrine she was staring at was only a few months older than Nolia was now. She had no idea that she'd die by her husband's hand after facing years of embarrassment and ridicule because of him.

Katrine had withstood much for the sake of tradition, for trusting that the gods had wanted Elias to win her Competition. It made Nolia's heart ache as she thought of Mikael and Isidore. She'd been queen for such a short time, and yet it pained her to know how far she'd been from being as strong as Katrine.

"The queen of Icaria has always been a Riona," Nolia murmured. "Candice picked my family herself to rule the queendom. There is no family greater than ours."

"You're wrong."

Justina grabbed the portrait, and it swung in, revealing an incredibly dark room.

"What in the gods' names?" Nolia blurted out.

Justina winked. "Would you like to see what your father was up to before you imprisoned him?"

• • •

Elias' spy office was small. There wasn't much room for the pine desk and bookcase that took up the entirety of the wall behind it, and the only decoration was a tapestry on the wall opposite the desk. But Nolia's eyes were on the door across from the one she and Justina had entered through.

"Looking for the last letter you sent?" Nolia asked as Justina rifled through the papers on the desk. She'd ignored the pile of books, but Nolia grabbed one. There was no one to stop her since Justina's rebels had remained outside by the portrait.

The mistake I've been waiting for them to make, Nolia couldn't help but think. She may not have been allowed very often in the king's chamber, but she knew her way around. Once Justina relaxed, she'd bolt out the door.

"I'm sure one of his little spies already destroyed it," Justina replied. "He had to be careful with what he kept in case of discovery, unlike me. I keep everything in case I need it later."

Like Isiris, Nolia thought.

"If you didn't work for my father and never had any plans to —"

"Why didn't I expose him?" Justina finished for her.

Nolia tried not to scowl as she nodded.

"Because he wanted you and your mother dead. If he killed you, that was one last thing I had to do. I'd only need to reveal that he was the one behind your deaths and the people would turn against him. They'd gladly welcome a new monarch with more rights than him."

Nolia flipped through a journal with one hand while the other cradled Katiana. She skimmed the neat handwriting that spoke only about what Katrine was up to, based on what she was able to understand.

"Why did you attack now?" Nolia asked. "If you wanted to wait until my mother and I were both dead by my father's hand?"

"He had his chance to kill you and he didn't," Justina responded. "It meant I had to take matters into my own hands."

Nolia set the journal down and reached for another book as Justina continued her search. "What are we looking for?" she asked as casually as she could manage. The new book was one about battle strategies, which she'd read before and had found quite boring.

Justina smiled but didn't answer.

Nolia moved onto another book, this one filled with maps of Icaria and the surrounding ocean. She frowned when she noticed that some of the Aecorian islands closest to the queendom had been circled.

Justina noticed her confusion and snatched it from her.

"Was that what you wanted?" Nolia asked, watching her carefully. "Is your niece in Aecoria or something?"

Justina's head snapped up, and the look in her eyes made Nolia wish she'd kept her mouth shut.

Nolia forced out a laugh. "I'm only kidding. I know how terrible things are between Icaria and Aecoria. We weren't allies before the war, and we certainly aren't now."

Justina slammed the book shut, and when Nolia tried reaching for another, she stopped her. "You think you're so intelligent," Justina said. "You think that you'll be able to get all of my secrets out of me before you run away. As if I wouldn't notice how you keep glancing towards that door."

Nolia's blood ran cold. "I'm not—"

"You are. I'm not an idiot, Nolia Riona." Justina's lips curled into a snarl. "No idiot would be succeeding at taking back a queendom."

"Don't you mean stealing?" Nolia answered. "I don't care if your niece is Candice herself. The Rionas were placed on the throne for a reason. Icaria is *mine*."

Justina's eyes flashed angrily, and she motioned widely towards the door. "Go on. Run along and open that door. See what's waiting for you."

Justina had spoken the words as if they were a threat, but a calm washed over Nolia like rain. *She's bluffing*, she thought. She didn't know how she knew that there wasn't any danger behind the door, but she did.

Nolia ran, throwing the door open to find no one waiting for her. It opened to a bedroom, *Elias'* bedroom. She didn't have the time to mock the bright green curtains or the gaudy gold bed sheets that he'd chosen before slamming the door shut behind her. It was a bookcase on the bedroom side, so she threw books to the ground to find the doorknob. Servant doors weren't supposed to be locked so that the staff could enter to clean or serve their employers without issue, but that didn't mean they didn't have locks.

The doorknob rattled before Justina began to pound on the door, screaming, "What are you doing? I told you that she was to remain unharmed!"

So she did *think there was someone in here*, Nolia thought, her eyes sweeping across the room before she saw that Justina was right. The crumpled bodies of two rebels lay on the floor, blood seeping from where they'd been stabbed multiple times. Droplets of their blood trailed to the wall to Nolia's right.

Justina's shouts continued as Nolia scrambled to the wall, pressing her fingers everywhere she could reach before the wall swung open. She stepped into the dimly lit passageway, shutting the door behind her.

Before she could decide which direction to go, something sharp pinched Nolia's side.

"Beatrix?"

Her father's mistress looked terrible, her hair a mess and her eyes rimmed with red. Nolia could see that bruises were also forming around her face.

"What happened?" she asked, keeping her voice down. She prayed that Katiana would remain quiet too. "You shouldn't be out of your room."

"My prison, you mean," Beatrix answered, her voice cracking. "Where you were going to keep me until I gave birth to your sibling."

Nolia genuinely hadn't decided if that would be the case or not, but she figured it was best not to admit it.

"What happened?" Nolia repeated. "What are you doing here?"

"Isn't it obvious?" Beatrix pressed the sword harder into Nolia's waist. Nolia realized with horror that it was stained with blood; Beatrix had been the one who'd murdered the rebels in Elias' room.

"The rebels found you?"

Beatrix nodded once. "They knew who I was. I don't think they knew about my baby, but they wanted me dead."

I'm sorry, was the first thing Nolia thought, but her tongue had gone numb. If the rebels had gotten to Beatrix, what did that mean for the nobles? For her family? Had the rebels killed her Uncle Kristopher and her cousins like they'd tried with Beatrix?

"You were supposed to be safe," Nolia mumbled. "We were all supposed to be safe."

"Well, we aren't," Beatrix snapped.

"You can put the sword down," Nolia told her. "I'm not going to harm you."

"How do I know that for certain? There's no one else here. You could kill me and when my body's discovered, pretend that it was one of the rebels. You would be free of me and this baby no one wants."

The sadness in her tone had Nolia wanting to apologize again. She may not have liked Beatrix very much, but bringing a child into the world wasn't something every woman was able to experience. It must have been difficult for her to be doing it alone. To feel like her baby was an inconvenience.

"Wait," Nolia said. "Do *you* not want your child?"

Beatrix shot her an irritated expression. "Of course I do. I don't have any family left."

Neither do I, Nolia thought, although she supposed it was a lie. She may not have ever been close to them, but she had her uncles and cousins. And she had Audrie, regardless of whose blood ran through her veins. Now she'd have a little brother or sister too.

"We need to work together to get out of here," Nolia decided. "Do you know which way it is to the servants' quarter?"

Beatrix scoffed. "I know your father may not have cared about the statuses of his previous mistresses, but do I look like a servant to you?"

Nolia wished they weren't in such a dire situation so she could tell her *yes* to spite her.

"Fine," she said instead. "Maybe if we go left, we'll—"

The squeak of a door interrupted her.

"A trap!" Beatrix shrieked, and Nolia only had a moment to think before shoving Katiana into the woman's hands.

"Run," she ordered. "Don't look back, and for the love of the gods, keep her safe. Prove that you're worthy of being a mother."

The words knocked Beatrix back a step, as if she hadn't thought that she might not be worthy at all. Then she nodded, bringing Katiana closer to her before sprinting away.

Nolia wished she'd asked for the sword before letting her go. And that she hadn't forgotten before now about the door underneath the tapestry in the spy office that Audrie had told her about.

Justina lunged towards Nolia, and she had no choice but to press her back against the dirty wall to avoid being sliced. When the rebel smirked, she realized that she hadn't been trying to hurt her. Only trap her again.

Why doesn't she just kill me? Nolia couldn't help wondering.

"Enough of this," Justina said before she could ask. "Any more tricks or games and Audrie will pay the consequence."

Nolia froze, never so distressed to be right before in her life. "*You* have Audrie?"

"Yes," Justina said. "Ready to be killed the moment I say so."

19

Audrie

ALONGSIDE THE ROYAL soldiers and Isiris' rebels were the knights. Audrie and her group were ushered past them to Isiris' tent some way from the tree where they'd run into her. She wanted to ask about them, but Isiris was too busy informing them about the forces they'd sent to the meeting point not far from there, and then Mikael poked his head into the tent and there was no longer any chance to ask.

"Thank the gods." Mikael threw his arms around Audrie and lifted her up.

"I see my lookouts aren't doing their job," Isiris commented. She looked as if she wanted to sit down, but the tent was void of any furniture. She was the opposite of Isidore, who shifted from foot to foot, eager to do anything but stand idly next to his mother.

"There's no need to be so dramatic," Audrie objected, wriggling until Mikael set her down.

"There is very much a need," Mikael said, his green eyes darkening. "We were terrified when we couldn't find you anywhere. When we found the letter from your father, we—"

"What letter?" Audrie interrupted.

Mikael grimaced as if he'd said too much.

"Don't mind him." Cilia had slipped in behind her brother, and she stepped towards Audrie next. She grabbed her head, moving it this way and that before looking Audrie up and down. "You're what's important. Are you injured at all?"

"No." Audrie smacked her hands away. "They weren't allowed to hurt me. I was their 'princess.'"

"Not everyone's," Darius said, crossing his arms. "It's a miracle those rebels didn't harm you. With all of the noise I heard, I could have sworn we'd be too late."

"Darius?"

Audrie turned to the tent's entrance where another knight had found his way inside: Rubin. He ran to Darius, jumping into his arms, and Audrie had to look away, not wanting to risk catching them sharing a kiss. She didn't think Darius was the type for public displays of affection, but they hadn't seen each other since the last trial. A kiss would certainly be warranted.

Cilia leaned closer to Mikael, keeping her voice low. "Are they —?"

"Yes," Audrie answered for him, keeping her eyes anywhere but on the boys. "But you didn't hear it from me."

Mikael raised his eyebrows at her. "So his feelings for you as 'Levi' weren't as shocking to him as I'd thought."

"Feelings?" Cilia repeated, her eyes widening. "He liked you when—?"

"I'd really rather not talk about this," Audrie begged, risking a glance at the boys—at Darius. Somehow she'd let her feelings for him grow stronger than they ever should have. Perhaps it was a good thing he was reunited with Rubin; now she could see the truth of his feelings for herself. Rubin was the one who had his heart, not her.

As if sensing her thoughts, Darius pulled away from Rubin and looked at her. His violet eyes seemed to be pleading with her; for what she wasn't certain.

"Levi," Rubin said, smiling kindly. "I'm glad to see you're alright too after hearing about your disappearance."

"I'm not Levi," Audrie reminded him, looking around the tent. "Levi's my brother, who isn't here?"

"He should be," Isiris said, her expression grim. "But he went with the group that was supposed to find you. He was adamant that as your brother, he had to go, and... I allowed it."

Isiris' gaze shifted to the ground, and Audrie knew she was thinking about her own sister. How she would have done anything to save Miri from what had happened to her.

"We've sent messengers to retrieve him from the meeting point," Isidore assured Audrie.

Mikael raised his eyebrows. "Not stop the fight altogether?"

"No," Isidore said. "They may no longer have Audrie, but Her Majesty would want us to capture them. Unless *you* know better what she would want?"

There was an accusation in his tone that had Audrie wincing. Isidore had apparently caught onto Mikael's feelings for Nolia.

"We need people at Candicia," Audrie blurted out before Mikael could respond. He didn't appear upset by Isidore's words, but Cilia certainly did, and the last thing they needed was to get side-tracked with an argument. "I know Justina is an important opponent to take down but—"

"Justina?" Isiris interrupted with a frown. "What about her?"

Darius let out a humorless laugh. "They don't know," he told Audrie. "They haven't figured out that Justina is the one behind all of this."

Isiris shook her head while the others shot them confused stares. "Justina is at Candicia," she said. "Not with these rebels that stole you."

"They're *her* rebels working alongside Elias' supporters," Audrie answered. "My father and his allies thought whatever she had planned for today was a distraction so they could break Elias out of the dungeon, but it isn't. Not when Justin already admitted to me that she doesn't want to make Elias king—or to let Nolia stay queen."

"We have to go to Candicia," Mikael said, terror washing over his face.

"Right now," Audrie agreed.

Isiris shook her head. "What are you two going to do? You're —"

"I'm their so-called princess," Audrie interrupted. "They won't hurt me."

"You're Elias' supporters' princess," Darius corrected again. "Justina already tried to kill you once. Do you want to give her the opportunity to try again?"

"I'm not going to die," Audrie snapped. "I'm going to save my best friend. Now are Mikael and I going alone, or will you give me some of your soldiers, Isiris?"

"I go where my brother goes," Cilia said.

"We'll go too," Lia spoke up, reminding Audrie that she and Meriah were also there. The spies had been doing an excellent job of keeping attention off of them until then, and Meriah looked incredibly irritated with her younger sister for ruining that, but she didn't contradict her.

"I'll lead," Isidore said, looking sternly at his mother. "Half of our people should do."

Darius groaned. "And naturally there's no way I can avoid being a part of this. Will you ever stop dragging me into danger, Audrie?"

Rubin hooked an arm through his. "This time she'll be dragging us together," he said, but it didn't placate Darius, and it certainly didn't Audrie.

She nodded to Isidore. "You can gather everyone while we get a head start. I'm assuming you have horses?"

• • •

Katrine had clearly wanted to keep her heirs close since they weren't far from Candicia at all. Audrie found it miraculous that no one had ever found them—at least not anyone who had lived to tell the tale.

When they reached Candicia, they headed towards the right to the same gate that Audrie had used as a prisoner since it was closest to the dungeon. That was where Audrie knew her father would be.

"Come on." Audrie dismounted before the dungeon's entrance, the doors already torn down.

"I don't think it's smart for us to go alone," Mikael objected from behind Cilia on the horse the siblings had shared. She'd insisted on taking the reins, resulting in quite a bit of squabbling between the two. "Especially when Isidore and his forces shouldn't be too far behind us."

"We can't wait for them," Audrie answered. "My father is in the dungeon right at this moment, trying to break Elias out."

Rubin shifted in the saddle as Darius followed her down. "How do you know it's your father?"

"It doesn't matter if it is or isn't." Cilia jumped off her horse. "*Someone's* in there and we can guess why."

"Still doesn't mean it's her father."

Audrie glared at the red headed boy. "How much do you want to bet I'm right?"

Darius stepped in front of her, the tips of his boots touching hers as he glared back at her. "My *life*," he snapped. "Because yet again, you're about to risk it."

It bothered Audrie more than she liked that Darius had defended Rubin. But of course he had. *Rubin* was who Darius cared about, not her. It certainly had never been her.

Audrie turned away as Mikael and Rubin also dismounted, going to the fallen door.

"Do you know where they're keeping him?" Cilia kept her voice down.

"No," Audrie admitted. "But I remember the general direction."

No one appeared reassured by her response, but they followed her inside.

"Should we have someone stay back as a lookout?" Mikael suggested. "Someone to not only warn about rebels, but also be able to tell Isidore where we are?"

"I volunteer Rubin," Darius said.

Rubin huffed. "You don't think I can take care of myself if we run into any trouble? I did fine in the maze and—"

Darius shut him up with a look. "You're the weakest fighter here. It makes most sense to put you in the position."

A pang pricked Audrie's side as they stepped deeper into the dungeon without Rubin. The phantom pain was duller than the last time she'd been there, but she gripped the hilt of her sword tighter in an attempt to ease it.

"Which way?" Mikael asked when Audrie hesitated after the first two intersections, the only ones she remembered.

"I'm surprised neither one of you has a map," Darius commented. "You're rather excellent at getting your hands on forbidden ones."

Cilia frowned. "What are you—?"

"Nothing," Mikael said, scowling at Darius. "I'll tell you later."

"I think it's straight," Audrie said.

"You think?" Mikael repeated.

"He's this way," Audrie insisted. "If you don't trust me, you can stay behind with Rubin."

Darius was the first to go after her, and Mikael and Cilia followed.

The group of four began to run, and at every intersection, Audrie tried not to hesitate long before plunging forward. Mikael asked over and over again "Which way?" and if it had been anyone else, she likely would have gotten annoyed. Instead, it only reminded her of the excitement of when they'd been about to find Nolia in the maze.

If only Audrie could summon an ounce of that now.

"I think we're lost," Cilia said. "We went in a circle."

"No, we..." Audrie spotted a cell they'd already passed. They all looked the same, but this one had the gods' names scratched into its walls. Why its previous occupant had used the sharp object they'd come across to do that instead of escaping, Audrie had no idea.

"I think I remember the way we came," Darius said. "I've been trying to keep track."

"Trying is different than doing," Cilia commented.

"I don't see you trying *or* doing."

Cilia's hands curled into fists, and Mikael touched her shoulder. "Let's backtrack," he said. "If this happens again, we should give up our search for His Majesty. The dungeon only has one exit, so all that matters is that we catch Audrie's father before he takes the king."

"Fine," Audrie said, but she knew she wouldn't be giving up. She wouldn't rest until she'd stopped her father.

They backtracked, turning left as a clang echoed through the dark and dirty space followed by a series of curses.

What was that? Cilia mouthed.

Audrie took off running silently, grinning to herself. *Keys*, she mouthed although no one could see her. Apparently, they'd only just missed Elias' rescuers.

"Where's the key?"

"Damn the key—break the lock!"

The last voice was Elias'.

Darius grabbed onto Audrie's sleeve as if to slow her down, but she shrugged him away.

The other voice had been her father's.

Audrie unsheathed her sword as she got to the hallway where Nolia had stopped so she and Isiris could talk to Elias without him seeing her. She knew she would have recognized the spot even without the bickering coming from her father and his lackeys.

"Audrie," Mikael hissed warningly, but she ignored him too, storming into Elias' hallway with her sword high.

"I told you, Father."

Seven men looked up at her, almost in a panic. Elias' face shifted into a glower while the man holding the ring of keys dropped it again, and Josip let out an almost hysterical laugh.

"Audrie," he said, "what in the gods' names are you doing here?"

"Stopping you, obviously." Audrie pointed her sword at the rebel leaning down to grab the keys. "Don't move."

"As if I'd listen to you," he answered, swiping them up. "You think you can take on six grown men?"

"Seven once we free His Majesty," another said.

Elias tried to puff his chest out, and Audrie rolled her eyes. The only thing she feared about fighting Elias was the possibility of him sitting on her.

"No one's hurting anyone," Josip said, glaring at his men. "This is your princess, have some—"

"She is *not*," Elias snapped. "She's your child, your pawn in all of this. The good news is that I may be more likely to forgive you for lying if you free me now."

Josip's jaw dropped, but he nodded. "Yes, Your Majesty." He took the keys.

"What do we do with her?" one of the rebels asked.

"Leave her be," Josip said. "You said so yourself that she can't take you on."

Maybe not alone, Audrie thought, feeling her friends nearby, but they still hadn't made their presence known. So she fixed her eyes on her father and aimed the sword. "Put the keys down or you can watch me try."

Josip pressed his lips into a firm line. "Audrie—"

She lunged—not at him, but at the rebel closest to her. He'd expected it, and easily blocked her blade before swinging at her himself.

"No!" Josip roared as another man scrambled to attack Audrie too.

She didn't know how she managed to stop him from slicing her through in time, but she did. She kicked the first rebel, sending him flying back onto his bottom.

The other men hooted teasingly at their fallen teammate, which only angered him further. He charged towards Audrie with new strength, so much so that she had to duck.

"I told you to—!"

"Let me out of here!" Elias bellowed. "Or I swear I'll kill your daughter myself!"

Audrie heard the clanging of the keys as she ducked again, avoiding one rebel while parrying the blade of the other.

That was when Darius chose to rush out of the hallway, heading towards the angrier rebel.

His eyes widened. "What—?"

The man wasn't able to finish his sentence as Darius had already stabbed him, the metal glittering in his back.

Audrie didn't linger on the moment, trying to use her opponent's surprise to her advantage. She cut his dominant arm and he yelped before lashing out at her wildly. Audrie easily dodged him, noticing his weak grip on the weapon. She'd injured him enough to win their fight so long as no one else joined against her.

But of course someone would. She and Darius were outnumbered four to two.

Where are Mikael and Cilia? Audrie wanted to scream as she parried the attack of another rebel. There was one rebel for each of them to fight, so why hadn't they come out with Darius? Aside from that, she'd also assumed that Mikael would be the one more likely to come to her defense. Had he and Cilia decided to turn around? But why would they?

"That's the one, now hurry."

"No!" Audrie shrieked, and with all of the strength in her body, she stabbed her opponent's stomach. She slid her sword back out, dodging another rebel to get to Josip. "Father!"

The cell door swung open.

Audrie heard more footsteps behind her, and she was able to process that their backup had arrived. But they were too late.

Elias sprinted past Audrie, going in the opposite direction of Darius and the others. She didn't know if he'd actually be able to escape that way, but she knew she should have followed him anyway.

Instead Audrie attacked her father.

Audrie raised her blade, and as Josip turned towards her, she brought it down, almost slicing through bone.

The keys in his left hand fell to the dirty ground.

Josip let out a scream that any other time would have hurt Audrie to hear. Instead she readied herself to strike again. Her father had taught her to be an honorable fighter, to never attack anyone that didn't have a weapon, but right now she didn't care.

"Audrie!"

Audrie kicked Josip back, slamming his body into the cell bars before she used the hilt of her sword to knock him to the ground.

"Audrie!"

Audrie positioned her sword, in her mind's eye seeing it cut his body in half, before she raised it above her head.

"Audrie, *no!*"

Someone seized the sword from her hands and they slammed down emptily. Her perfect hit had been taken from her.

Josip collapsed onto his side, pale as he held his bleeding wrist tightly to his chest. He blubbered incoherently.

Audrie whirled around, ready to scream at whoever had taken her sword.

"Audrie," Levi said, his palms bleeding from where he held the blade. "What are you doing?"

"Levi!" Audrie knocked the sword away and took his hands, the blood making her head spin. She lifted her skirt to press the fabric to his palms, her body trembling. "Why would you do that?"

"Because he's our father. How could you try to...?"

Levi trailed off, but Audrie knew what he was questioning.

How could she try to kill their father?

The same way I murdered our brother.

Tears sprang to Audrie's eyes as the guilt engulfed her anew.

"He betrayed us," she said. "He kidnapped me and kept me prisoner, he planned a rebellion to free Elias, and he... he *disowned* me for power."

Sobs escaped from her throat, and Levi wrapped his arms tightly around her. "He'll get his justice," he promised, "but it doesn't have to be by your hand."

"Levi, don't you understand?" Audrie tried to pull away from him, but he wouldn't let her. "He succeeded. He freed Elias."

Levi shook his head. "He didn't," he said.

Audrie turned in the direction Elias had gone. "He...?"

Levi offered her a weak smile. "Mikael and some of the other soldiers were already waiting for him on that side," he said. "It turns out your friend is very good at making plans."

20

Nolia

WITH JUSTINA'S BLADE pressed to her back, Nolia made her way downstairs. They only went down one flight before Justina urged her in a new direction, and Nolia questioned who had shown Justina her way around Candicia. They clearly hadn't done a very good job.

Justina led Nolia into a long hallway that was purely decorative. It didn't lead anywhere, instead offering a beautiful view of the garden with floor to ceiling windows, and large portraits and grand-looking mirrors adorning the walls.

The fading light made it difficult to see now, but Nolia spotted a large group loitering on the grass, and she almost asked Justina what her rebels were doing there.

That was, until she noticed they weren't alone in the hallway.

"Have you been watching carefully as instructed?" Justina asked the figure. "Who are they?"

"They're Isiris' people. I spotted her son among them. I left to warn one of your soldiers to tell others, but that was some time ago, and no one's done anything."

"They must be busy," Justina said at the same time Nolia gasped. Not from the surprise or excitement that her friends were there to help her. But because she recognized the voice of who Justina had gone to meet.

"Calix?"

The boy stepped away from the window, evidently shocked to find her there when he'd only been expecting Justina.

"Nolia," he breathed out.

She hadn't seen him in days, not since Mikael had knocked him unconscious and tied him up to be dealt with later. She hadn't asked about him, assuming he was locked away in the dungeon while she dreaded his inevitable execution.

"You know each other?" Justina asked, a hint of amusement in her tone.

"Yes," Calix said, and it was all Nolia needed to see how he longed for her. The regret that shone in his eyes—regret that she knew wasn't because of what he'd done to her. All Calix regretted was that she'd found out and it'd ruined things between them.

But maybe she could convince him differently.

"I'll take care of them," Justina told Calix, eyeing the rebels distastefully. "Find someone else to inform me if Elias is freed."

Justina pressed the sword into Nolia's side to move her along, and she flinched away from it. "Wait," she said, trying to force her voice to break. "Can't you let me speak with him? One last time? I know I'll never see him again if you take me."

"No," Justina snapped as Calix answered, "Of course you'll see me again."

Nolia laughed humorlessly. "No, you won't. She's going to kill me after she kills my father. She wants Icaria for herself."

Calix sucked in a breath as Justina grabbed Nolia's arm tightly. "Shut up," she hissed. "He's not going to help you."

"Please," Nolia wailed so terribly, she almost winced. "Don't I at least deserve to say goodbye to my love?"

"Love?" Justina repeated, the word rolling off her tongue in disgust.

"Love?" Calix echoed, his expression conflicted, and for a moment Nolia was worried that he wouldn't believe such a blatant lie. Then she saw how brightly his green eyes were shining. "You don't love me," Calix said. "You never said it before, and now, with every-thing—"

"Of course I love you," Nolia interrupted quickly. "You told me that I was impossible not to love, do you remember? Well, so are you. I won't deny that you've hurt me terribly, but it's been in more ways than you thought. It pained me to know that I'd fallen in love with you when I could never marry you like I dreamed. That's why I didn't tell you when I realized it, I didn't want you to share in my despair."

Nolia was out of breath, and her back was starting to hurt from how hard Justina was jabbing the sword at her so she'd walk, but she remained perfectly still. She forced herself to keep her gaze on Calix, to keep her eyes soft and vulnerable. Like a silly girl who was finally revealing her feelings.

"For the love of Mirah, *you* were the boy in the secret relation-ship with her?" Justina shook her head at Calix. "You're not actual-ly believing any of this, are you?"

"What reason would I have not to believe the truth?"

Nolia nearly wilted from relief. The hope in his eyes had been plain from the moment she'd begun to speak, but she'd been afraid he would laugh at her attempt to seduce him into helping her.

"Especially," Calix added as he pointed his sword at Justina, "when you didn't deny that you're going to betray His Majesty."

Justina tensed, raising her own weapon from Nolia's back, and it was all she needed to break away from her. She sprinted to Calix, Justina's sword on her heels.

"You dimwit!" Justina screamed, preparing to strike. "She's only—"

Calix's sword met hers in time to stop it from stabbing his head.

Even in her anger, she wasn't going to hurt me, Nolia couldn't help but notice.

Calix shoved Nolia behind him before blocking another swipe.

"She's going to run away!" Justina shrieked.

"Of course she won't." Calix nicked her arm. "She'll wait until I'm finished with you."

Nolia inched towards the closest door to her, watching the dance between the rebels, as she tried to decide what the best plan was. The palace had likely been overtaken by the rest of Justina's rebels, making getting to Isidore a dangerous feat. She didn't know where any of her guards would be to escort her—other than her room, and she couldn't go back there no matter how terribly she wanted to. Giana's blood still stained her hands and the bottom layer of her gown that she hadn't torn off.

So what else could Nolia do? Was Calix her best chance at surviving long enough to find her friends?

Calix let out a pained cry, and that was when Nolia formed her plan. If he was her only chance of salvation, he couldn't lose the fight.

Nolia raced around them, making her largest circle around Justina so that her blade couldn't touch her.

"What are you doing?" Calix shouted at her.

"Running away, isn't it obvious?" Justina responded. "I told you she was pretending."

Nolia stopped in front of a small mirror on the wall, prying it off its hook before lifting it over her head.

Since Justina's back was to her, Calix saw what she was doing first, and quickly stumbled away. He kept his sword ready to defend against Justina, but she was too confused to attack.

Justina began to turn around. "What—?"

Nolia launched the mirror at her. She watched it shatter against her skin, the tiny pieces leaving a multitude of scratches as glass flew in every direction.

Justina crashed to the floor, and Nolia raced over to her. She grabbed her sword with one hand while checking with the other that the rebel was alive.

"Nolia, you beautiful genius." Calix swept her into his arms, catching her by enough surprise that she dropped the sword. She hoped he didn't notice her wince as the metal clanged through the hallway.

Calix's lips found hers, and for a moment, Nolia allowed herself to enjoy the feel of them. They were the only other lips she'd ever be able to kiss that weren't Isidore's. The only lips that she'd chosen to press to her own.

Or at least she'd thought she'd made the choice.

Nolia pulled away, scooping up the sword as she glanced at Justina's fallen body. "We need to tie her up," she said. "Get her somewhere no one will find her. Perhaps hit her over the head again to be certain she won't wake up for a few hours."

Calix gave her an odd look. "Why would we do that?" he asked-ed.

"Justina's our most infamous rebel," Nolia reminded him. "Although I suppose my father may make a close second once historians start writing about all that's happened the past couple of years."

"His Majesty would kill anyone that referred to him as a rebel," Calix replied. "He's the king, nothing more and nothing less."

This time Nolia gave him an odd look. "Are you going to help me or not?"

"No," Calix said. "We're going to the dungeon, finding your father, and asking for his blessing."

"His blessing?" Nolia repeated. "Why would we need—or *want*—that?"

"To live," Calix said simply. "If you're agreeable, signing over your right to the crown to him before disappearing forever, he'll have no issue allowing us to marry."

"Marry?" Nolia was beginning to feel like a parrot.

"Yes." Calix took her free hand. "Isn't that what you wanted, Princess?"

He stared at her, so wide-eyed and hopeful that it almost hurt Nolia to tear her hand away. "I'm not a princess anymore, Calix. I'm queen." She used her stolen sword to rip a thick piece of fabric from her gown to tie around Justina's wrists and feet. "I'm not going to leave Icaria and the people I love to live with you in secret."

"I thought I was one of the people you love."

Nolia stood to stare at him, at his handsome face and his tousled hair that she'd run her fingers through on several occasions, at his bright green eyes that she suddenly found herself wishing were a darker shade.

Jade, she thought. *Like Mikael's.*

Nolia raised her sword. "How could I ever love someone that spied on me? That didn't try to save me when he knew I was supposed to die? That still now, doesn't believe that I should be queen?"

Calix didn't move, his eyes hardening. "So you lied?" he asked. "About everything?"

"Not everything," Nolia answered. "Justina really was going to betray Elias."

Calix's hand curled into a fist at his side. "I didn't lie," he told her. "I do love you despite trying hard not to. I want to marry you and have children with you. I want *you*."

"You should know I'm engaged," Nolia replied. "To Isidore."

Calix flinched. "I don't see a ring."

"It's not public knowledge." Nolia slipped the ring out from under her bodice. The metal was warm to her touch and the bluish-purplish gem shone in the faint light pouring through the windows.

"Do you love him?" Calix asked. "Is he who you won't leave behind?"

"No," Nolia scoffed. "You know me better than to think I'd stay for a boy."

"Right." Calix smiled faintly. "I always thought that it was the idea of your future husband that I was fighting for your heart. But it was Audrie all along, wasn't it?"

Nolia tightened her grip on her weapon. "There's no love truer than the one between best friends."

"There is," Calix said, releasing his sword so it clanged to the marble floor. "Because in a moment like this, a friend would hurt you. I won't."

Calix lunged at her, wrapping his arms around her and lifting her over his shoulder before he began to run down the hallway.

"Stop!" Nolia shouted, the sword slipping from her grip, so she grabbed it with both hands. "What in the gods' names are you doing?"

"Exactly what I told you I would. We'll get your father's blessing, and then we'll leave."

"Are you insane?" Nolia shrieked. "I'm not going to marry you —put me down!"

"Never."

If she weren't out in the open for anyone to find, Nolia wouldn't have minded leaving Justina where she was. But she needed to hide her before finding a place to hide herself until she could get help.

In order to do that, Nolia knew she'd have to get rid of Calix.

Nolia tightened her grip on the sword before digging it into Calix's thigh. He cried out, crumbling forwards onto the floor, and landing mostly on top of her. She pushed out from under him to remove the blade from his leg, and he screamed again.

"Quiet! Someone's going to hear," Nolia said, holding the bloodied sword in both her hands. She trembled as she stared between it and Calix's leg, unsure if she should try to stop his bleeding.

Calix flipped onto his back, staring at her in disbelief. "You stabbed me," he said. "You don't love me, do you?"

Perhaps a part of me does.

Nolia tore off another piece of her gown, cringing at how ruined it was. It had previously hung down to her ankles and now was shredded to her knees, with splatters of blood.

"Don't." Calix touched her wrist as she reached for his leg. "Just kill me."

"Kill you?" Nolia repeated, her face twisting with horror. "Calix, how can I—?"

"Kill me," Calix interrupted. "Or I'll have no choice but to kill *you*."

He was suddenly on top of her, pinning her arms above her head with one hand while the other reached for her neck.

"Calix, no!" Nolia screamed as he pressed down on her throat. She lifted her leg to knee him between his legs.

Calix grunted, falling sideways, giving Nolia the opportunity she needed to scramble back. She didn't look at him again until she had a firm grip on her sword.

"You said you wouldn't kill me." Nolia tried to get to her knees.

"That was before you *stabbed* me."

Calix pounced at her again, but this time Nolia stuck her sword out, trying to force him to stop. But even if he'd tried, he would have been too late. The sword plunged into his chest.

"Calix!"

Nolia watched his eyes widen as he noticed the sword shoved through him before he collapsed onto his side.

"Calix, no—I'm sorry." Nolia moved him onto his back, not removing the sword this time. She didn't tear off any pieces of her skirt, simply pressing what she could into his chest as the blood continued to pour out of him.

"Calix, please," Nolia begged as one of his hands rested itself over hers and his eyes fluttered shut. "I'll find a physician, I'm sorry, I didn't mean to, I never wanted—"

But he was already dead.

• • •

When Audrie found her, Nolia hadn't moved from where Calix's body had fallen. She'd pulled him into her lap and removed the sword when it became clear that he was gone. The reasonable part of her mind told her that it was necessary to have the weapon ready in case she needed it, but Nolia wasn't certain she could have used it if she'd tried.

She'd killed someone. She'd taken a life, and it hadn't been anyone's. It had been Calix's. Someone she'd known. Someone she'd had affection for. Someone she should have never been fighting in the first place.

"Nolia?" Audrie gently placed her hands on her shoulders.

Nolia's body was so numb, she hardly felt her. She'd only known that her best friend had arrived because she knew Audrie would come eventually. Someone in Isidore's group would have seen her and told her.

"Nolia, it's safe now," Audrie tried. "Mikael captured your father and—"

"I tied up Justina," Nolia said. "So she's taken care of too."

Audrie swallowed. "Did she kill Calix?"

"No. I did."

Audrie knelt next to her. "I'm sorry," she murmured. "That couldn't have been easy, killing someone you loved."

I didn't love him, at least not very much, Nolia almost answered, but when she looked at Audrie, she kept the thought to herself. Audrie wasn't talking about her and Calix, and she knew it.

"Do you think the gods will forgive us?"

Audrie avoided her gaze. "If one of us deserves to be forgiven, it's you."

Nolia was about to tell her that she deserved the same when she saw a flash of movement out of the corner of her eye. "Stop!" she shouted, turning to stare down the hall at where she'd left Justina's unconscious body.

Mikael and Cilia straightened, holding their hands up as if in surrender.

"It's only us, Your Majesty," Mikael said.

"We wanted to check if she was alive," Cilia added.

"Of course she is, I didn't kill her too."

The siblings grimaced, and Nolia felt a rush of guilt. Her own pain was making her lash out, and they didn't deserve the brunt of it.

"I'm glad that you're alright," Nolia said, glancing back at Audrie. "What about Levi? And Isidore and Isiris and—?"

"I only know about the people that came to Candicia," Audrie said. "But yes, Levi and Isidore are unharmed. So are Darius and Rubin."

Audrie mentioned the last two with uncertainty, as if she didn't know whether or not to be glad they were fine. Nolia decided not to comment on it, but kept her question about it for another time.

"Has anyone checked on my household?"

"That's where I wanted to go since Yadira insisted on staying behind," Cilia answered.

Nolia straightened. "Yadira was injured," she remembered. "So was Giana, and who knows how many others. They'll need a physician."

"And we're laying around here?" Cilia motioned towards Mikael to help her with Justina. "We need to get to her—them—*now*."

Nolia swallowed. "What about Beatrix and Katiana? Has anyone heard about them?"

"We haven't," Mikael said quietly.

Nolia looked down at Calix's body, brushing a lock from Calix's forehead before forcing herself to stand. Audrie kept a hand on her elbow as she did. Nolia knew the gesture could make her look as if she were too weak to stand on her own, but it didn't matter because it was the truth. Nolia needed Audrie and she always would. People would have to get used to it.

"We'll find them," Audrie promised her. "There should be enough soldiers around to focus on more than keeping your father and Justina captured."

Nolia nodded. "We won't need them for long," she said. "They'll be executed tomorrow."

Audrie stiffened, and Mikael nearly dropped Justina. "Don't you need to be crowned first?"

Nolia's heart was beating so loudly in her ears that she hardly heard him, but even if she hadn't, she would have known what he was thinking. She knew Audrie and Cilia were wondering the same.

"I can't afford to wait until my coronation," Nolia said. "If this rebellion has taught me anything, it's that I can't keep stalling. My father and Justina, and all of the rebels opposing me, need to die."

21

Audrie

WHILE NOLIA INSISTED, the execution wasn't ready to be held until three days later. The day before she would officially be crowned Queen of Icaria.

Audrie had watched Alexie try to talk Nolia into waiting every day since the decision, but the teenage queen refused. Isiris always offered her approval, despite not having been asked for it, and no one else spoke up. Not even Audrie, since she didn't have an opinion.

At least not one about Elias' fate.

"Are you afraid?"

Audrie kicked up the blankets, trying to find her way back to Nolia in the enormous bed. Eventually she settled onto her right side so she could see Nolia calmly staring at her in the dark.

Audrie knew the sun was likely rising, and she hated that Nolia's room had no windows. But it was supposedly safer for the queen to sleep in a windowless room where guards could more easily stop an intruder from murdering her in her sleep.

Not that it had helped Katrine, but Audrie would never mention that.

"Afraid of what?"

"For your father," Nolia said. "For his sentencing."

Audrie had been trying not to think about Josip, and thankfully no one had brought him up. Levi certainly hadn't, and she presumed he'd told Cecily since she'd been carefully avoiding the topic, despite her many tears. She and Nolia hadn't discussed him either since she'd recounted what had happened. But she'd known that Nolia and her council were issuing judgments on the rebels. Almost all of them would be dying.

"No," Audrie said. "I know what he deserves."

"I know you think you do," Nolia sighed, "but I hate that you would choose to be fatherless."

"I already am. He disowned me himself."

"He didn't, he—"

"He was being selfish, Nolia, and I could have died. What sort of father does something like that?"

"Mine did," Nolia said. "But he isn't like yours. Elias never loved me."

Audrie stared at Nolia's unblinking eyes. It pained Audrie that Josip could have loved anything more than he did her, but Nolia spoke matter-of-factly about Elias' lack of affection towards her.

"Maybe when you were a baby he did," Audrie offered.

Nolia gave her a small smile. "I haven't been a baby for a long time."

Before Audrie could come up with a response, there was a knock on the door.

"Your Majesty? Are you awake?"

Nolia sat up, glaring at the door. "Yadira, go back to bed or I will strangle you. The physician said you need to rest for three days, so don't be an idiot and make it six."

"I feel perfectly fine," Yadira complained through the door. "It's only a concussion."

Audrie knew her struggle, and rubbed the back of her head. She liked to think that she was completely healed, but the doctor had warned that it would take time.

"Yadira."

"Fine, I was only waking you so the others could start getting you ready."

"Let them in." Nolia stretched before glancing at Audrie. "Let's go get pretty to kill some rebels."

• • •

Prior to this one, Audrie had only ever attended one execution— Nolia's. She'd been awoken with a start, having barely slept the night before from a combination of guilt and illness from the poison she'd ingested. Meriah hadn't told her where she was going, only to get dressed and go.

Then she'd been led outside to find her father and brother waiting in front of the stage with other nobles. It hadn't been until Nolia was brought out that she understood what was happening.

This execution was much more straightforward.

Nolia gingerly stepped onto the stage her father had attempted to murder her on, standing tall as she faced the crowd. It had been moved closer to the dungeon so that there would be a clear line from its door to the stage.

The crowd continued to murmur, its number larger than the one that had attended Nolia's since there'd been more time to invite people. Most had accepted, not wanting to miss watching their former king die. That or they were looking at the execution as the opening ceremony for the coronation festivities.

A hand brushed Audrie's shoulder, and she looked at Levi, who was prone to feeling nervous within large crowds. But he wasn't touching her, busy whispering something into Cecily's ear next to him.

Audrie craned her head around to see that Darius had gotten permission from the guards surrounding her family to come near her.

"What are you doing here?" Audrie asked.

Darius scowled. "Hello to you too."

"Shouldn't you be with Rubin and the other knights?"

"Rubin went home with them," Darius answered. "You didn't hear that Her Majesty freed them?"

"No." Audrie frowned, wondering why Nolia hadn't mentioned it. "Why didn't you go with him?"

"Her Majesty invited me to attend her coronation."

Audrie would have shot Nolia a glare if she knew she'd see the look.

Darius shrugged. "Besides, I have nothing waiting for me at home."

"You have Rubin."

"Actually, I don't." Darius focused his gaze on the stage. "He's no longer—as you loved to refer to him—my boyfriend."

Audrie's head swam with questions, but the one she blurted out was, "Isn't that what he was?"

Darius didn't reply.

"Welcome," Nolia said, and the murmurs died down. "Ordinarily a queen would not speak before an execution, and ordinarily a queen would also need to be anointed before executing her enemies. But today I break with these traditions because there are words you need to hear, and because these aren't just my enemies, they're *yours*."

The crowd was completely silent.

"With all of my heart, I want to be a good queen, to be what Icaria deserves," Nolia continued, clasping her hands together. "In order to be that for you, I need to be certain that my reign will begin peacefully and without issue. The death of these traitors will bring not only that, but safety throughout Icaria." Nolia paused, her gaze hardening. "They will be examples to any and all rebels that may appear in the future. They will know what their fates will be if they dare go against me and attempt to harm my people. I will show them no mercy, as these traitors will not be shown it either."

A shiver went down Audrie's back, and she wished she'd paid better attention when Nolia had been practicing her speech.

"So understand me, and let the word spread that Nolia Riona, Queen of Icaria, will not gently restrain those who terrorize Icaria like her mother, and will not encourage rebellion like her father. I will listen to your complaints if you come to me as a loyal subject, but the moment that you become a rebel, your life will no longer be your own. It will be mine to end as I see fit."

A wave of uncertainty washed through the crowd. Some bowed their heads in respect while others trembled with fear. And still there were those who didn't seem to know whether or not to take their young queen seriously.

Audrie could see the passion in Nolia's eyes telling her that they should.

Nolia stepped away from the stage and was placed in a seat off to the side to watch, as the monarchs typically did at executions. It was an odd tradition in Audrie's opinion, but then again, it was odd to have the power to sentence anyone to death.

The rebels were brought out one by one, beginning with the least important ones: Justina's rebels, who had been captured within the palace. They'd been given the option to swear themselves to Nolia, but had declined. So they all lost their heads in single swings.

After some time, Audrie stopped watching, and she could feel the crowd growing impatient. She only glanced up every now and then to be certain that her father wasn't next. And to see Nolia, her unflinching gaze as the ax went down.

"I don't see Mikael, do you?" Darius' breath tickled Audrie's ear. "Do you think he may have been too weak-willed to come?"

"Not everyone enjoys death as much as you do," Audrie snapped. "Besides, I think he's keeping Yadira company."

Darius frowned. "The lady-in-waiting? Cilia is with her."

Audrie frowned back at him. "How do you know that?"

"I saw them on my way here."

Audrie sighed. Nolia wouldn't be happy to hear that Yadira was refusing to rest. She'd mention it to her later, and try not to laugh when Nolia likely tied the girl to her bed.

Any amusement at the thought swiftly disappeared when Audrie spotted Justina. The rebel leader had joined the execution line with no way out of it.

Why is Justina dying before Father?

Audrie had expected him to be close to last in line since he was one of Elias' confidantes, but he wasn't more important than Justina. If Audrie had organized their order, she likely would have placed him right before her. It was odd that Nolia wouldn't have... unless she intended to make some sort of statement in regards to him?

Audrie's stomach began to twist itself into knots as Justina was dragged onto the stage and no one was brought out behind her.

The crowd murmured with excitement, many pleased to be seeing the infamous rebel for the first time. She was calm, going as far as to smile at her audience, until she was at the block where she would lay her head.

"Let me speak!" Justina shouted.

The crowd's excitement grew, and Audrie found herself curious too. What could the rebel possibly have to say now that she was about to die?

Nolia motioned with her fingers for the guards to ignore Justina, and they wrapped a black piece of cloth around her head to cover her eyes.

"Icaria is not yours!" Justina screamed. "Icaria is Aecoria's!"

Audrie's heart stopped, and people around her sucked in their breaths in shock. Aecoria had almost attacked Icaria years before, during Queen Katrine's Competition, because of their belief that Icaria wasn't meant to be an independent country. Kalama, the kingdom of Uri, the sun god, had come to Icaria's rescue, resulting in a years-long war that had left the Aecorian royal family and a great deal of their people dead. As a result, Audrie had been taught that Aecoria no longer existed.

But clearly that hadn't been correct.

"My death will only be a temporary solution!"

Justina's upper body lay perfectly on the block, her neck stretched for the executioner as she turned her head in Nolia's direction. "You may be rid of me, but mark my words, Nolia Riona," she warned, "it won't stop the true queen from taking the throne. Moselle will return and she will kill you!"

The ax dropped.

Audrie flinched, and so did Nolia.

Moselle? Who is Moselle?

The crowd whispered to one another, questioning whether or not Justina was telling the truth or simply trying to scare them. Audrie thought that the latter made sense since desperate people would say nearly anything, but she could see that her best friend thought differently. In fact, Nolia looked as if something had been confirmed for her.

Audrie wished that she could ask, that she could push her way through the crowd to sit next to her and gossip for the rest of the execution.

Except that Audrie realized that she wouldn't want to speak at all for the next execution as Levi edged closer to her. He wrapped one arm around her shoulders and the other around Cecily.

Darius gave them an odd look before he realized what they were waiting for. He patted Audrie's arm awkwardly, which didn't make her feel any better, but the attempt was appreciated.

The crowd's voices grew louder until the dungeon doors opened again, and out stepped the next person to be executed.

Elias.

Audrie tore away from her brother, a shout in the back of her throat. Levi grabbed one of her arms, and Darius the other, both boys holding her back as she tried to catch Nolia's attention. Her voice was gone, but she knew that Nolia would be able to read her eyes, to know what she wanted to scream.

Where is my father?!

Nolia watched Elias be blindfolded and kneel before the block, her hands primly resting in her lap. She kept her expression neutral, but Audrie could see the anger sparkling in her eyes, the part of her that was eager for him to die.

"Long live the queen!" Elias called out, mockery in his tone. "A murderer as much as her mother was."

Audrie went limp, and Levi and Darius kept her from crumbling.

Elias' head and body were dragged away, and the crowd began to disperse, following their silent queen's lead. The execution was officially over, and Josip was alive somewhere.

Before Audrie could chase after Nolia, one of the guards protecting her family turned towards her. "Audrie Girard," she said. "Your family's presence was requested in the throne room following the execution."

• • •

Nolia was already waiting for them with Josip, his wrists tied together with Isiris next to him, holding tightly onto the chain. The former rebel looked as if she wanted to kick him despite the solemn way he stood, having clearly not said anything to her to warrant the violence.

But Audrie knew exactly how she felt.

While her brother and mother bowed and curtsied, Audrie stormed forward the moment the doors shut behind her. She glared at Nolia, unbothered on the throne that she wanted to drag her out of. If they'd been alone, she may have tried.

"What's going on?" Audrie demanded. "Why isn't he dead?"

Josip cringed at the harshness of her tone. "You wish to see me dead that terribly?"

"Was the last time we saw each other not enough evidence for you?" Audrie snapped.

Josip's fingers stretched to gently touch the wrist that she'd tried to cut off. She imagined that the thick bandages around it didn't make the chain also clasped there hurt any less.

"We're not here to argue," Nolia said, giving Audrie a pointed look. "We're here to sentence Josip Deirdre."

"We already know what he deserves," Audrie said, crossing her arms. "That's why we were prepared to watch him die."

"I know." Nolia leaned forward in her chair. "But it's because I love you as much as I do that I decided differently. Despite the monster that my father is, you wouldn't have executed him publicly if you knew it would hurt me. I won't do that to you."

"You think that a private execution is *better*?" Levi asked, raising his eyebrows. "You think that we'd like to watch him die at all?"

"Of course you don't," Nolia replied. "That's why you won't."

Audrie relaxed. *Nolia brought us here to say goodbye*, she thought. It was the sort of thing she'd think to do, possibly because she wished she'd been able to do the same with Corinne or Katrine.

Audrie set her gaze on her father, trying to smile. He would pay for his sins, but at least now her family wouldn't have to watch. He could die alone in his cell or wherever else Nolia wanted. It was what he deserved after all he'd done to tear her family apart.

"Josip Deirdre is to be sentenced to a lifetime in a prison of my choosing."

Audrie's head whipped back to Nolia. "No! Are you insane?"

"She's your queen, you probably shouldn't call her insane," Levi said despite the disbelief on his face.

"I don't care," Audrie said, stomping closer to the platform before pointing at Josip. "She's insane if she thinks that allowing him to live is a smart decision."

"He'll be locked away," Nolia told her. "He won't be able to harm anyone ever again."

"How can you sincerely believe that? Elias' supporters are still out there, and they may try to break him out."

"He's not important enough for that," Nolia said. "Besides, those people will be taken care of rather swiftly. Isiris and your spy friends are cooperating nicely."

Audrie hadn't seen Lia or Meriah the past couple of days, but she was glad to know they were doing alright after all the trouble it took to get them to help Nolia.

"What about the Moselle girl Justina brought up?" Audrie asked. "He knows something."

"I don't," Josip said with a frown. "Who's this Moselle?"

Nolia waved the question away. "I've already made my decision, and there are very few people who are aware of what it is. Even less will be allowed to know where Josip will be imprisoned."

Isiris laughed humorlessly. "It'll be a better kept secret than where Miri and my nieces stayed."

Audrie didn't know how she could possibly joke about *that*, but she kept her attention on Nolia. "Please," she said, "just kill him."

Nolia smiled at her sadly. "If I do, you may someday grow to hate me—or worse, yourself."

She stood then, making her way down the steps to stand in front of Audrie. Nolia held her hands out, waiting for her best friend to take them, and after a moment, she did.

Nolia kept her voice down as she told her, "You already carry so much guilt about Alaric. I can't let you carry this burden too. It may kill you, and I couldn't go on without you."

Audrie's eyes welled up with tears, so she blinked quickly and squeezed her hands.

"If you hide him away, does that mean we won't be allowed to visit?"

"You can." Nolia looked at Levi. "Whenever you wish. You need only ask me to arrange it. You'd also be free to live with him."

"Live with him?" Audrie repeated, dropping her hands. "Why would we want to do that?"

"She means me," Cecily said, stepping forward.

"You?" Josip asked. "You would want to live with me in prison?"

"Husbands and wives should live together, shouldn't they?"

Josip shook his head. "We're not—"

"You are," Nolia interrupted. "Elias was never the actual king of Icaria, and his council wasn't a legitimate one. Their dissolvement of your marriage was invalid."

"But if you believe otherwise, consider this a proposal." Cecily kneeled, staring him directly in the eyes with an intense gaze, her eyes clearer than they had been in days. "Josip Deirdre, will you marry me again?"

Josip stared at her, speechless. "We were hardly married the first time."

"Then let's be genuinely married this time," Cecily answered.

Josip continued to stare at her, a whirl of questions in his eyes. Audrie imagined that hers looked quite similar—although she didn't think hers held quite as much hope.

"Say yes, you fool," Isiris told him. "Or do you believe you'll find a more beautiful woman dumb enough to follow you into an eternal imprisonment?"

Cecily's cheeks pinked, but she smiled shyly. "Well?"

Josip leaned down, taking her hands so that she would stand. "Yes," he said. "There's no one else that I would rather be banished with."

They kissed, and Audrie didn't know whether to look away or continue staring because she'd never seen them do that. The only affection she'd ever witnessed between her parents had been that of kind words and stares. She'd only ever seen her parents act as friends, people who knew everything about each other after years spent together.

But perhaps it was on that friendship that they'd built something stronger.

"I'd like for us to be remarried," Josip said, glancing at Nolia. "Even if we are technically still married."

Nolia smiled back at him before nodding. "I'll call for Agnesia."

22

Nolia

IT WAS BITTERSWEET watching Audrie's parents together. Nolia couldn't help but wonder if she'd find as much joy with a person. To have enough love to follow them into an uncertain fate.

Nolia didn't think she ever would. She loved Audrie more than anything, but she'd refused to run away with her during the Competition. Likely no other love would ever compare to that, so she'd have to continue on, living cluelessly.

But Nolia tried not to think about that as she left the Girards to spend time together as a family—and to find Yadira. Her lady had been healing steadily, according to the physician, but Nolia had still been trying to check on her personally, and now seemed like the best time to do so.

No matter how desperately Audrie's eyes had pleaded with her to stay. *She needs to be with her family*, Nolia told herself. She knew that Audrie was simply unsure how to feel about the changes in her family dynamic, and she needed to come to terms with that with them.

Nolia first looked for Yadira in her room, and the guards swiftly informed her that she'd gone to Nolia's chamber to dine in the tea room. Why she would do that, Nolia had been confused about, until she got there and found Yadira eating with Cilia.

"Your Majesty, I hope you don't take offense to my being here," Cilia apologized. "I didn't want Yadira to be alone."

"That's alright," Nolia replied. "I didn't want her to be alone either."

A third chair was added to the table for Nolia, and she sat between the girls, drinking a chalice of wine that one of the maids insisted on bringing her. She should have asked for tea since she would be having plenty of wine at the party the next day, but she couldn't help herself. She took small sips as the girls finished their dinner of chicken, brown rice, and roasted vegetables.

"I should go," Cilia said once Yadira's plate was empty. "I told my family I wouldn't be gone very long, and I don't want them to worry."

Yadira's face fell, and it made Nolia hesitate to let Cilia leave. "Thank you for keeping Yadira company," she said. "I'm glad to see how much of a liking you've taken to her."

Cilia blushed. "She makes it difficult not to like her."

Nolia tried not to envy Yadira for getting along with Mikael's family as the girls said their goodbyes. "Have you met the rest of Mikael's family?" she asked once Cilia was gone. "They should all be here for the coronation."

"I haven't," Yadira said. "Perhaps Cilia will ask if they want to meet me before they go."

"I would think Mikael should be the one to do that," Nolia commented. "Seeing as how he's the one courting you."

"Right."

Yadira's voice cracked awkwardly, and Nolia glanced at her. "What?" she asked. "Is something wrong?"

A maid appeared with two slices of lemon cake, smiling brightly as she placed the large pieces onto the table. "Enjoy, Your Majesty," she said with a curtsy. "My lady."

Nolia would have laughed at the size of them if she wasn't so concerned by the look on Yadira's face. She waved the maid away.

"The thing is, Your Majesty..." Yadira took a deep breath. "I don't know if you'll be upset with me."

Nolia frowned. "What did you do, Yadira?"

"It's not what I've done, it's what I'm going to do," Yadira bit her lip, "which is to tell you that I don't think I want a husband."

You don't want a husband? Nolia wanted to blurt out until she thought about it, and it wasn't much of a surprise. She'd never spoken kindly about marriage, and Yadira had never tried to convince her differently. She must have become as disillusioned as Nolia was by the idea.

"I think I may want a wife."

"A wife?" A giggle escaped Nolia's lips at the absurdity of Yadira's words before she saw the seriousness in her gaze. Nolia gasped, covering her mouth. "Cilia?" she said, the realization dawning on her. "You're in love with Cilia!"

"I don't know if it's love, but I'd like for it to be," Yadira admitted, her cheeks red. "I'd like to be with her instead of Mikael."

"Oh my gods," Nolia mumbled, shaking her head. The girls had been spending so much time together that it should have been obvious. *But what about when Yadira met Mikael?* she thought, remembering the bashful mess Yadira had become; the exact way she acted whenever one of the handsome noble boys paid her attention. She swiftly realized that Cilia had been there too.

"It was never Mikael that you liked, it was Cilia from the beginning," Nolia mumbled. "And I thought I'd done so well pairing you together."

Nolia didn't add that she'd been miserable about the matter. Especially since now she felt *worse*. How was she going to tell Mikael that she'd failed to find him the love he desired? She could only pray that his sister's happiness would make the blow less painful.

"Mikael is a great boy," Yadira assured her. "I may have grown to like him if it weren't for Cilia or..."

"Or?" Nolia asked drearily. She didn't know if she could stand to hear what else the most perfect boy she'd ever met was missing.

"Or if he didn't already have feelings for someone else."

Nolia nearly jumped out of her seat. "He likes another girl?" she exclaimed. "Who? Did he tell you? How do you know? Who is she? How—?"

"Your Majesty."

Yadira winced, and Nolia shut up, so as not to cause her a headache.

"The other girl is *you*."

Nolia stared at her, lips parted as her mind attempted to process Yadira's words.

The other girl is me? Mikael has feelings for me?

"How do you know?" Nolia whispered.

Yadira appeared alarmed by her quiet response. "Whenever I spend time with him, all he talks about is you," she said. "Then there's the way he looks at you... like you're the sun, moon, and stars."

Nolia's heart swelled, but she shook her head, trying to remain logical. "He could talk about me because I'm something the two of you have in common, and I'm his queen, so that could be why he would look at me with so much—"

"No," Yadira interrupted. "He has feelings—romantic feelings —for you. I think he only courted me because he thought it would please you."

It didn't please me, Nolia thought, unable to fight a smile. *Not at all.*

"Your Majesty," one of her guards approached her.

For a moment she looked to Nolia like Giana, and her smile slipped away. Poor Giana, who hadn't deserved the death she'd suffered. Nolia curled her hands into fists, remembering her blood all over them.

"Many guests are arriving for the coronation," the guard went on. "Prince Thiodore says that you requested you be summoned to greet them."

Nolia sighed, rubbing her temples. She'd made no such request; her uncle had simply pointed out that greeting guests was the correct thing for her to do.

"Don't worry about me, you should go," Yadira said, swiftly picking up both slices of cake. "I'll finish these and take a nap."

Nolia's head snapped up. "Yadira."

Yadira was already halfway out of the room, clearly desperate to escape, but she stopped, her shoulders stiffening. "Yes?"

"Thank you for finally being honest with me."

Yadira visibly relaxed and she glanced over her shoulder to give Nolia a small smile. "I'm trying to be better at that," she answered.

"Good."

Nolia watched her leave, knowing that she should go too, but she couldn't make her legs work. She needed a moment to herself. A moment to simply *think* before she was surrounded by too many people to do so.

It was unsurprising when Nolia's thoughts drifted to Mirah. She'd felt inclined to ask for Mirah's intercession during the attack, and so she had. They'd won the battle, but was it a result of pure luck, or had Mirah answered her prayer?

Remain with me, and I will remain with you.

The words came to Nolia suddenly, and she couldn't remember where she'd heard them. All she could recall were a pair of unsettling blue eyes.

"Your Majesty?"

The guard was waiting to escort Nolia to greet guests, and Nolia shook her head.

"I need a moment," she said, her voice cracking. What she needed was a distraction, something to calm her before she went to whatever chaos awaited her. She certainly wouldn't find that with her own muddled thoughts about promises and inhuman eyes.

Nolia spotted the perfect diversion on one of the side tables by the tea room's couches, somehow unscathed after all that had occurred there. She strode towards Katrine's book, lifting it up by its seams so it flapped open for a moment. It was long enough for a paper to slip out. At first Nolia assumed that it must have been a bookmark. Until she realized that it was too wide and that there had been something scrawled on it.

214

It looked to her like a letter.

"Your Majesty?" the guard asked again as Nolia kneeled on the cold marble floor.

"Leave me." Nolia waved away her concern. "I'll let you know when I'm ready to leave."

She heard the guard's boots thump away as she stuck her head underneath the couch, reaching so far that her shoulder nearly cramped.

With the paper now in her hands, Nolia straightened, about to sit on the couch when she spotted her name on it.

Nolia's hands began to tremble. The letter was for *her*.

Dear Nolia,

I write this the night before the final trial of your Competition. My mother did the same for me, and so I thought it only right to do for you.

I admit that I don't quite know what to tell you. At our conversation earlier when you escaped the tower, I said most of what I'd been intending to tell you here. I wanted to remind you about the sort of queen that you should be since you'll be reading this before your coronation. Instead, I find myself thinking about you in this moment, not years from now as a grown woman with a husband and children. Try as I might, I can't seem to see you as anything else. So I suppose I'll talk to you as I see you.

The Competition was a gift from the gods, from Candice herself. She wanted to give anyone the ability to become king and father the next queen. She wanted kings to come from different parts of the queendom with diverse backgrounds. She wanted the monarchy to reflect Icaria as a whole.

The reservations that you hold are not unwarranted. The marriage between your father and I has never been healthy, and I've heard the gossip plenty of times. I've seen you question our union as I did today. The truth of the matter is simple: I trust the gods. I knew that they would provide me with the husband that I needed.

However, it was not always easy to trust. There were many times that I was plagued with so much doubt that I spent countless nights begging the gods for understanding.

When you were born, I thought that I understood. I thought that all of the ridicule and barren years I'd faced were for you. The tiny healthy daughter I'd always desired to give my country. But then you began to grow, and while on the surface you took after me, I began to see Elias. I saw why the gods had picked him to be your father.

Where I was gentle, you were hard like him. When I cared what others thought, you disregarded their opinions as he does. Who I found difficult to trust, you could easily give your heart to as he always has.

Somehow all of the qualities that I'd hated in him, that I'd thought were flaws, suddenly weren't. The gods had meant for them to be passed down to you, to make you the strong queen that you need to be. So while now I see you as a fifteen-year-old girl, afraid of what the Competition will do to her life, I know that you will find the good in it. I know that you will see your knight, the first boy into the tower, and you will love him. You will have the partner that I never did because you will work to make him such. You will make Icaria better because you will give our people what I didn't: a true king to help you lead and balance the responsibilities of the throne.

I know a part of you, the stubborn nature that both your father and I gave you, may insist that you can do this on your own. But the truth is, you can't. I've tried for the entirety of my reign, and while I have no regrets, it isn't something that I want for you. You may exist to rule Icaria, but your life should not entirely be spent ruling.

So trust yourself, Nolia, and above all else, trust the gods. We were hand-picked to be Icaria's queens and so have our husbands been. We are what they wish to make of us.

Sincerely,

Your Mother

Nolia reread the letter multiple times, her heart pounding faster and faster until she let go of it, watching it float down to her lap.

Katrine hardly ever wrote anything personally, normally too busy to do so. But she'd taken the time to write this for Nolia. An incredibly important letter that Katrine would have given to Corinne or someone else that was supposed to be alive when Nolia ascended the throne. Instead, she'd kept it wedged between the book she'd been reading, thinking she had time.

Although perhaps subconsciously Katrine had known differently. Maybe it was why she hadn't been able to imagine a version of Nolia so far into the future. Why she'd left the letter somewhere Nolia would have the chance to read it, only before she was crowned.

It felt like too much of a coincidence to not have been planned by the gods.

The gods worked in mysterious ways, but this was something that Nolia knew she needed to understand. She reread the letter another time, searching for what it was that not only Katrine was asking from her, but the gods.

So trust yourself, Nolia, and above all else, trust the gods.

Nolia had always been a devoted person, interested in learning about the gods and praying often. Despite how little they knew each other, Katrine must have known that about her since Corinne wouldn't have raised her any other way.

So why had Katrine put such a strong emphasis on it? Why would she—why would the gods—think that Nolia was lacking conviction?

The answer struck her like an arrow, the shock and fear nearly making her fall over.

Nolia clutched the letter to her chest before going to the tea room door to the guard still patiently waiting for her.

"I need you to inform Isiris and Isidore that I need to speak with them," Nolia told her, "and that it can't wait a moment longer."

23

Audrie

AUDRIE COULDN'T CELEBRATE. How could she be happy that her parents were together—*genuinely* together—after everything that had happened? After their selfish plans had not only resulted in her being kidnapped by rebels but ended in her murdering her own brother?

Her parents—her father—needed to receive justice for what they'd done. But instead, all they would receive was banishment. The strongest punishment that Nolia would give because she didn't want Audrie to regret anything.

And Audrie hated herself for being grateful.

Cecily and Josip wanted to celebrate their reunion in their room, but Audrie left the throne room before they could beg her to join them. She went to her own bedroom, storming inside. She needed to yell at the wall, to stab something with a sword, to—

"Audrie."

Audrie nearly screamed, spinning around, the sword already in hand that she'd been about to dismember her bed's pillows with.

A shriek was met by her action, followed by a laugh that only served to infuriate her.

"What in the gods' names are you doing in my room?" Audrie hissed.

Lia and Meriah had appeared out of nowhere, now standing out of her sword's reach at the end of her bed, but all it would take was one lunge for Audrie to harm either one of them. It didn't look as if either girl was armed, but Audrie knew better than to trust that.

"Don't tell me you're here to announce that you're kidnapping Darius *again*," Audrie said.

"After how well it went the first time? I think not," Meriah replied.

Audrie's grip tightened on her sword. "Then what are you doing in my room?"

"Can you put that thing away?" Lia asked, evidently having been the one who'd screamed.

"Not until you tell me what you're doing here."

The sisters glanced at each other, as if silently deciding who should speak.

Finally Lia stepped forward, clasping her hands in front of her. "We're here to thank you," she said, "and tell you that we want to stay."

"Stay?" Audrie repeated, raising her eyebrows.

"Yes," Meriah said. "Assuming that the offer still stands after we've finished helping Her Majesty with her rebel problem?"

The sisters had spent the past few days with Nolia's guards cleaning out Elias' old spy office and identifying the remaining rebels within the palace. They'd also brought files and other things from the house where Audrie had been kept prisoner that they were supposed to be going through. She didn't know how much longer the work would take, but Nolia would want them to be thorough.

"Can I ask what made you change your mind?"

The words had escaped Audrie's lips before she could think too much about it, and the sisters paused, glancing at each other again in another silent conversation.

Meriah reached for her younger sister's hand, her dark hooded eyes turning to Audrie. "We have nowhere else to go," she admitted quietly. "His Majesty... Elias gave us our only home after our parents died."

Audrie could tell that it was difficult for her to say, and it suddenly made sense why the sisters had avoided Audrie's question about how they'd come to work for Elias. "You were orphans," she murmured. "That's how you became spies?"

"We would have been thrown out otherwise," Lia answered, her gaze downcast.

"Of the palace?" Audrie asked. "Were you a normal maid and guard before?"

"No, the daughters of them," Meriah said. "Elias wanted us to take up their positions after they passed."

Audrie wasn't entirely certain, but she knew that the sisters were around her age. They'd been old enough that they could have been working while their parents were alive, but they must have been paid an abundant amount for it not to be necessary. Something that wasn't all that common for staff.

Audrie looked at the sisters more carefully. "Did Elias want you to replace your parents as more than just a maid and guard?"

Lia inched closer to Meriah, and Meriah tightened her grip on her sister. Neither one spoke, but Audrie had her answer all the same.

"A family of spies," she commented, shaking her head. How many more were there like their family? She hoped that Lia and Meriah would be able to find them all for Nolia.

"After what your parents have done, I wouldn't be one to judge," Meriah pointed out.

"Besides, we weren't really a family of spies," Lia added. "We never did any sort of work for Elias until..." She swallowed. "It was about a year ago," she told Audrie. "After Nolia's fourteenth birthday."

"They ate the venison," Audrie realized with a gasp. Alaric had brought Nolia a deer he'd shot and killed from a hunting expedition with his father as a gift that had made anyone who'd taken a bite sick. A good chunk of the staff that Nolia had shared her birthday meal with had died as a result. To that day, Nolia was still convinced that her brother had poisoned it.

Now Audrie couldn't help but be certain it hadn't been Alaric behind the plan, but Elias.

"Neither one of us likes the taste," Lia said.

"It's the only reason we were saved since we ate everything else," Meriah added.

"I'm sorry," Audrie told the sisters, despite knowing that the words couldn't have meant very much. Not after the terrible loss they'd suffered, only to be put at the mercy of the man who'd been the reason for it.

"Don't give us your false condolences," Meriah answered, although Audrie could see that she appreciated the words. "Swear that you'll let us stay, working for the queen now as opposed to her father."

Audrie raised her eyebrows again. "I thought that you needed to hear that sort of thing from Nolia directly?"

Meriah shrugged. "You've proven that your word will do."

Audrie cracked a smile. "Then I swear."

The sisters nodded, the tension in their shoulders that Audrie hadn't noticed before dropping.

"Only if you stay away from my brother," Audrie added on a whim, her gaze flitting to Lia.

Lia pursed her lips. "Seriously?" she complained, her cheeks pinking as her eyes grew defiant.

"No," Audrie said. "He likes you for whatever inane reason, so I won't interfere—unless you hurt him. Then there *will* be a problem."

Lia gave her a smug smile. "Should I call you 'sister' now?"

If there'd been anything safer than a sword to throw at Lia within Audrie's arm length, she would have done so. "Get out of my room!"

"Fine, fine. You should be with your parents now, anyway."

Audrie almost asked how they knew she was avoiding them, but she supposed she shouldn't have been surprised. Not when they were not only spies themselves, but had been the daughters of them.

"I'll let you know when I've spoken with Nolia," Audrie told them as they slipped through the secret passageway. She'd have to see about finding someone who could lock it from her side; the last thing she needed was for the sisters to keep popping into her room uninvited.

"You don't have to worry about that right now," Meriah said, shutting the door with a bitter smile on her lips. "Just... be with your family, Audrie."

• • •

Being with her family was much easier said than done. Audrie had been standing outside their room for at least ten minutes, sucking in deep breaths as she tried to find the courage to enter. The multitude of guards had been staring at her, some with concern and others in annoyance, but no one had spoken a word to her as she paced. Not until she stumbled in front of the doors.

"Are you finally ready to enter now?" one asked.

No, Audrie thought as she nodded. The guards opened the doors, and she forced her feet to move before she could think twice about it.

Audrie hadn't known what to expect when she entered her parents' chambers, but she certainly hadn't thought she'd see anyone that wasn't a member of her family. Instead, Beatrix stood in the middle of the room, grasping her mother's fingers with a panicked expression.

"What's going on?" Audrie asked.

"Audrie." Cecily seemed relieved to see her. "You're here."

Against my better judgment, Audrie wanted to say, but glanced around instead. "Where's Levi and Father?"

Cecily bit her lip, nodding towards the door across from her. "In his room, explaining to some guards how he escaped."

"Hm." Audrie stepped closer. "What does *she* have to do with any of that?"

"Audrie," Cecily scolded her for the disdain in her tone.

"You know who she is, don't you?" Audrie asked before she could go on. "She was Elias' mistress. He was with her when he was making promises of marriage to you."

"I know." Cecily sighed, unwinding her fingers from Beatrix's. "Then...?"

Cecily motioned Audrie to come over, so she did, albeit hesitantly.

"I was much younger when I found myself in your position," Cecily spoke, wrapping an arm around Audrie. "And I was terrified of what would happen to my child and me."

Audrie swiftly realized that it wasn't her that her mother was speaking to, and she watched Beatrix carefully, the woman bunching up her dress's fabric around her stomach.

"You had every right to be. He's dead now," Beatrix said. "By his own sister's hand."

Audrie flinched, and Cecily tightened her grip around her as if trying to garner strength from her.

"He's dead because his fathers and I made a mistake," Cecily said, her voice hoarse. "You won't do the same."

"You think that not attempting to claim the throne will keep us alive?" Beatrix was clustering so much fabric to her stomach that her dress was almost to her knees. "Nolia hated her father. She's going to hate this baby just as much if she doesn't kill us first."

"She wouldn't do that," Audrie said. They hadn't discussed how Nolia felt about the idea of a new sibling, but she knew that Nolia would never harm a baby, even if that child was Elias'.

"She would, she will," Beatrix insisted, her body trembling. "My family is dead, and so is this baby's father. There's no longer anyone left to protect us."

"It's going to be alright," Cecily tried to soothe her, reaching for her. "You're exhausted and afraid after what the rebels tried to do to you. You need to rest not only for your own sake, but for your baby's."

Beatrix melted into Cecily's arms, allowing herself to be led out the door. Cecily murmured more reassurances to her as they went, one of which Audrie was fairly certain was a promise that Audrie would speak with Nolia about the matter.

"What's wrong with her?" Audrie asked when the door clicked shut.

Cecily didn't move, her back to Audrie and her fingers on the doorknob. "The rebels—who were supposed to be Elias' allies—almost killed her," she said quietly. "Can't you see why she may be afraid that others may now attempt the same?"

Audrie frowned. *Maybe if I didn't know Nolia*, she almost said. Her best friend had been wracked with guilt over what the rebels' attack had done, and she would be doing all she could to keep everyone in the palace safe from now on. That would include Beatrix and her child.

"When I became pregnant, I was convinced that Katrine would want me dead as well."

Audrie looked up, her mother's back still to her. "You were?"

"Yes," Cecily said, the word empty. "Elias wasn't any help since he was too busy telling anyone with ears that I was pregnant. I spent the entire nine months terrified that someone would appear to murder me at any moment—and the fear didn't dissipate after Alaric was born. I didn't find any form of peace until I married your father."

Audrie didn't tell her that she understood why, that she'd once felt as if she never had anything to worry about when her father was around. Not when that was no longer the case, and she wasn't sure if it ever would be again.

The door to Josip's room opened, and he, Levi, and a large number of guards spilled out.

"I hope that's all you need, so you can leave me to my honeymoon?" Josip was asking them.

Levi snorted. "A honeymoon with two children won't be much of a honeymoon."

Josip shrugged. "It isn't as if we didn't already have Alaric for our first one." He turned towards the rest of the room, almost immediately spotting Audrie. "You came," he said.

Relief overfilled Josip's eyes as he spotted her, and he stepped forward as if he wanted to rush across the room to hug her, but Audrie in turn took a step back. Her lips wavered, trying to form the semblance of a smile. Someday she hoped to be able to forgive him for all he'd done, even if that day couldn't be today.

Audrie nodded, looking her family in the eyes. "I'm here."

24

Nolia

IT TURNED OUT that mother and son hadn't been doing anything for the coronation like Nolia had assumed. Instead, Isiris and Isidore were in her bedroom, playing a game of cards with a chalice of wine in hand—well, in Isiris' hand. Isidore's was on the table, completely full as Isiris downed hers.

The first thing she did when Nolia entered was pour another chalice.

"Sit, join us." Isiris offered it to her. "Don't be upset when Isidore wins. He's old enough now that he can beat me even when I'm sober."

"I've been beating you for years now, Mother," Isidore reminded her as he scooted a chair out for Nolia.

"Yes, since that year we hid in Kalama," Isiris agreed with a grin.

Nolia raised her eyebrows. *So the mainland was where you went,* she couldn't help but think. She supposed she should have assumed, but it was nice to have it confirmed.

Isiris poured herself more wine. "Do you remember that prophecy everyone was discussing?"

"Prophecy?" Nolia repeated. Kalama was known for having priests gifted with precognition. She'd heard about some of their predictions—like how the current king and queen would have twelve sons—but never about a prophecy.

"Don't mind her, she's drunk," Isidore apologized. "I would have told the guard that I'd meet with you privately, but... I knew you would need both of us." He avoided her gaze, staring at his full chalice, and Nolia realized that he already knew why she was there.

It should have made it easier, and yet it didn't. Nolia still had to force herself to get the words out. "I'm here because we need to end our engagement."

"What?!" Isiris nearly dropped her chalice. "You cannot—!"

"We can," Isidore interrupted, grabbing her arm. "Let her speak."

"No." Isiris tore her arm away and stood. "This is your future we're talking about. I've done everything since Nolia came fumbling into our lives for *you*, so that you could be king."

"I know," Isidore said, glancing down. "But you should listen."

"No," Isiris repeated, her nostrils flaring as she glared at Nolia. "Has my son not proven himself to you? He's been nothing but kind and understanding, you ungrateful—"

"Mother!" Isidore shouted, pulling her forcefully back into her chair. "You can't speak to her that way. She's our queen."

"She was supposed to make you king," Isiris told him, gripping his arm.

"No, she wasn't." Isidore hesitantly met Nolia's eyes. "Because I didn't win her Competition."

Nolia's lips parted. He understood better than she'd thought.

"This isn't about that," Isiris hissed to her son. "It's about Mikael. She likes him better than you, and she's using the Competition as an excuse to marry him instead."

Isidore looked at Nolia, as if daring her to tell his mother differently. So she sat up straighter, narrowing her eyes at her aunt.

"This *isn't* about Mikael," Nolia said. "He only 'won' my Competition because he cheated. He and Audrie used a map to get to the tower before anyone else. Then he wasn't going to come inside, but Corinne died and..." Nolia's voice broke, and she tried to blink back the tears that were forming at the memory. "The point is that if it had been an ordinary Competition, he would have been eliminated."

"All the more reason for you to marry Isidore," Isiris said. "Since if you wish to hold another Competition, there isn't a tower for you to do it with. You're the first queen in all of Icaria's history who has the excuse to marry whoever she wishes."

Nolia thought of the tower crumbled outside of the palace, its stone still littering the ground since everyone had been busy with Elias and Justina's rebels. But now they were gone. All of Nolia's enemies were gone.

"The tower *will* be rebuilt," Nolia told Isiris.

"How long will that take?" Isiris answered. "Can you afford to wait years to marry and begin having children?"

"I already have an heir, one that I won't treat the way my mother did Miri and your nieces." Nolia willed her to see the honesty in her eyes. "Katiana will remain at Candicia with me, being raised as the crown princess. Her existence isn't a threat to me, it's a *blessing*. She's given me time to figure out how to be a queen before I ever have to worry about how to be a wife or mother."

Isiris pressed her lips into a firm line, staring at her so intently and so soberly that Nolia wondered if she'd really had that much to drink. "As the person who conducted the engagement ceremony, I refuse to undo it," she declared.

Nolia froze. She hadn't thought about what she would do if Isiris didn't agree, and she *needed* Isiris' agreement. Only the person who had joined Nolia and Isidore could separate them.

"Actually you're going to do it," Isidore said to his mother, "because I don't want to marry Nolia either."

Nolia didn't know who gasped louder, her or Isiris.

"What do you mean you don't want to marry her?" Isiris snapped. "She can make you—"

"I don't want to be king." Isidore slammed a hand on the table. "I never wanted to be, but you never asked. You simply made your plan, and I had to go along with it."

Isiris appeared utterly shocked. "You didn't have to."

"I did. You wouldn't have helped her otherwise."

Nolia was speechless, her mind filled with too many questions. *What boy wouldn't want to be king? Why else would you want to help me? What did you want instead of marriage?*

"Is there someone else?" Isiris asked.

"No." Isidore appeared surprised by the question. "I've never had anyone to care about in that sort of way. I did try with Nolia—Her Majesty—but..." He shrugged, giving Nolia an abashed smile.

"No offense taken," Nolia assured him. "I may not like you romantically, but I do think you're a great friend to have."

Isidore's smile grew. "As are you."

He reached under his shirt to pull out the gold chain that her mother's ring was hooked onto. He began to unclasp it when Isiris lunged across the table to stop him.

"Mother, we're ending our engagement whether you like it or not," Isidore said, trying to shove her hands away. "We don't—"

"You need to do it *properly*," Isiris interrupted. "You cannot return the rings without the ceremony. Otherwise you'll remain engaged, and you'll become bigamists whenever you marry." She blinked, the effects of the wine coming back into her eyes. "At least that's what I think will happen, I'm not certain. Either way, your spouses will likely be upset about the situation."

Nolia nodded as if she'd known all along. Truthfully, she'd never attended an engagement ceremony, much less an undoing ceremony. Which she supposed was odd since nobles arranged and undid engagements often, depending on whether or not they could find their children more influential matches or if they'd fallen out with the family they'd wanted to join.

"We'll need Mikael." Isiris eyed Nolia. "As your witness, he swore to do all in his power to get you to the altar. Now we'll need him to justify differently."

• • •

Mikael looked as if he'd run to Isiris' bedroom, his cheeks flushed and chest heaving. His panic was palpable, and Nolia didn't have the chance to calm him before Isiris was already talking.

"Isidore and Nolia are ending their engagement," she said flatly. "Now stand by and say 'I do' when it's your turn."

Mikael's eyes only grew larger, and he looked at Nolia, a question on the tip of his tongue, but again there was no time.

"Join hands." Isiris motioned impatiently towards Nolia and Isidore before beginning, "Isidore, son of Isiris, despite your previous promise to this witness and the gods themselves, do you wish to end your engagement to Nolia?"

Isidore nodded. "I do."

"Nolia, daughter of Katrine, despite your previous promise to this witness and the gods themselves, do you wish to end your engagement to Isidore?"

Nolia looked at Isidore, who smiled encouragingly at her before nodding. "I do."

"Mikael." Isiris turned her gaze on him. "As the original witness of their promise, do you swear that it is in these two people's best interest to end their engagement?"

Mikael stared at Nolia, his eyes still questioning what they were doing before he answered, "I do."

"You may return your rings."

Nolia let go of Isidore's hands to unlatch her chain and slip the ring onto her palm. Once Isidore had done the same, they picked ed the rings up and placed them into the other's hand.

Something inside of Nolia shifted, as if a sword that had been hovering over her heart had finally been knocked away. She looked at Isidore to see if he'd felt it too, but he just seemed happy to have his ring back.

"The gods have released you of your promise," Isiris said. "May you find who your true life partner is meant to be."

Nolia slid the ruby ring onto her finger, admiring it before Mikael cleared his throat.

"Is anyone going to explain to me what happened?" he asked, his eyes again on Nolia.

So trust yourself, Nolia, and above all else, trust the gods.

"Yes." Nolia met Mikael's gaze. "But there's something else I'd like to do first."

. . .

Nolia hadn't attended very many feasts or balls, seeing as how she was supposed to remain mainly out of the public eye until she married, but she'd had many pretend ones with Audrie at Dismund Palace. This one wouldn't be like those at all.

The room was dark, with only enough light for the musicians practicing in the corner. They stopped when Nolia stepped inside with Mikael in tow, but she swiftly motioned for them to continue. Their harmony flooded over her, calming some of her nerves.

"This is where you wanted to talk?" Mikael asked, glancing around.

"Yes." Nolia wondered now if it'd been a silly idea.

"It's nice," Mikael said, which Nolia knew was a lie since it was not only half-decorated, but too dark to see anything. "Thank you for wanting to share this with me."

Nolia couldn't help but smile despite the return of her nerves. "Will you do me the honor of being my first dance partner as queen?"

Mikael's jade green eyes brightened. "Of course, Your Majesty."

"Nolia," she reminded him before they stepped onto the dance floor. She offered him a hand, and he took it easily, squeezing her fingers. The other she placed on his shoulder while his settled on her waist.

"What is it you wanted to discuss with me?" Mikael asked as he stepped forward and Nolia back, following his lead.

Nolia bit her lip. "It's about Yadira."

"I've been meaning to visit her." Guilt washed over Mikael's handsome face. "I'm sorry, I haven't been the most attentive suitor to your friend, but I will try to do better."

Nolia winced, hating the genuineness in his tone. "It's not about that."

Nolia twirled away from Mikael, and when she returned to his arms, he asked, "Have I done something wrong?"

"Absolutely nothing," Nolia answered, almost adding that she didn't think he could ever do anything wrong, but biting her tongue in time. "It's just that Yadira and Cilia would like to court."

Mikael let out a surprised laugh that was so quiet Nolia merely felt it reverberate through his chest. "I should have known," he said. "Cilia only pays that much attention to a girl when she likes her."

Nolia's feet followed his in a box step. "You're not upset?" she asked.

"Of course not," Mikael replied before he noticed how intently she was staring at him. "I hope you don't take offense to my lack of heartbreak over the matter. Yadira is a nice girl but—"

"She isn't me?"

Mikael stopped, and if there had been other dancers, someone certainly would have knocked into them.

"I—I don't know what you mean," he stuttered out.

But Nolia could see it in his eyes. What she'd been too blind to see until Yadira had allowed her.

"Don't lie," Nolia murmured. "I want to hear the truth."

Mikael continued to stare at her unmoving, so Nolia took his hand. She took the lead this time, and his feet followed.

"Did Audrie tell you?" Mikael whispered. "I should have known she'd—"

"Audrie?" Nolia interrupted. "She knows?"

Mikael blinked. "She didn't tell you?"

"*Yadira* told me."

Mikael stumbled, but Nolia kept him upright. "I was a horrible suitor. No wonder she'd rather be with my sister."

"You weren't horrible," Nolia objected. "You simply weren't meant for each other. I turned out not to be as good of a matchmaker as I'd thought."

"You're perfect in many other ways," Mikael told her.

Nolia's heart fluttered at the compliment, and she had to steady herself to respond. "Not when it comes to being honest. Otherwise, I would have never let you court Yadira."

"You wouldn't have?" Hurt flashed across Mikael's face. "Why?"

"Because *I* have feelings for you, Mikael."

Hope bloomed in Mikael's eyes, but he seemed to be trying to contain it. "You don't have to say that to be kind," he murmured. "You're my queen, and regardless of your emotions, I will serve you loyally."

"I'm not saying it to be kind," Nolia promised. "I'm saying it because it's true. I was wary of you at first, believing you were only helping Audrie and me because you wanted the crown to owe you a favor. I thought you were like every other boy who'd come to the Competition to further themselves. But you aren't, you're sweet and honest and caring—and handsome too."

Mikael twisted her so that her back was to his chest, their fingers interlocked in front of her as they followed the back-and-forth steps of the dance.

"I didn't come to the Competition to marry you," Mikael said breathlessly. "It was impossible for the idea not to cross my mind, but I knew there was another purpose for my coming here. I never meant to feel what I began to after Audrie was captured and we got to know each other. I was upset with myself for having allowed it to happen because you were never supposed to be mine. You were meant to marry someone else, whether it be Isidore or—"

"The first boy in the tower?"

Nolia felt Mikael's heartbeat quicken. "Yes," he whispered.

"That was you," Nolia reminded him.

"I cheated," Mikael answered. "And besides that, your entire Competition wasn't set up to find you a husband, but to find Elias an army of worthy fighters. It didn't count, you said so yourself that it didn't."

"But what if it did?" Nolia spun back around to face him. "You know about Calix, how long I was with him, but I never felt anything as close as I do for you. It was easy to control my emotions with him, it was easy to remind myself that he wasn't going to be my husband. But it wasn't with you, even when my husband became a real person through Isidore. I couldn't stop what I felt." She gripped his hands tightly. "What if our feelings aren't accidents like we thought? What if it's what the gods always meant to happen?"

Mikael squeezed her hands back just as tightly. "It would mean there's no need to hold another Competition," he said. "It would mean that you think I'm supposed to be your husband?"

Nolia had spent so many years avoiding the thought of having a husband. Corinne and many others had tried convincing her that she had no reason to worry, but she'd never believed them. She'd thought that the Competition would bring her as disastrous of a marriage as that of her parents'. But Nolia knew that if she married Mikael, it wouldn't be a disaster. It would be wonderful, and marriage would be a blessing to her as it was for so many others. She would be happy, yet that thought didn't erase her fears entirely.

"I don't know about who you're 'supposed' to be, but I do know I'm not ready to have a husband quite yet," Nolia admitted. "I'm afraid this isn't anything as certain as a marriage proposal, but it is one to be with me."

Mikael stared at her, his expression unchanging for a moment before he let go of one of her hands to raise the other to his lips. "I hope it isn't a marriage proposal because I wouldn't have accepted one anyway." He kissed the back of her hand gently. "You don't need a husband to be queen, Nolia, you don't need anyone. But if you want me, regardless of anything else, that's all the certainty I could ever ask for."

Nolia beamed, her heart surging with happiness, and when Mikael grinned in return, she threw her arms around his neck. She hugged him as tightly as she could and Mikael surprised her, lifting her off her feet and swinging her around in a circle.

"That's not part of the dance!"

A giggle escaped Nolia's mouth, and Mikael set her down, his grin having become sheepish. "I'm sorry," he said. "If you'd like for me to be more proper, I'll—"

Nolia stopped him, pressing a finger to his lips. "Mikael," she said, raising onto her tiptoes. "I'd like for you to kiss me. Assuming you don't mind having an audience for our first kiss?"

"Not if you don't." Mikael's cheeks were incredibly red, but a dopey smile appeared on his face before he leaned down.

Mikael's kiss was nothing but a brush against Nolia's lips at first, his shyness showing. Then he pressed his lips to hers more firmly, and she felt how perfectly their mouths fit together. It was as if she'd been made to never kiss anyone else but this handsome, wonderful boy in front of her.

"I should probably escort you to your rooms soon," Mikael murmured when he pulled away. "For propriety's sake."

Nolia laughed, cupping his face in her hands. "It isn't as if there's anyone to scold us about the matter."

Mikael's cheeks warmed under her palms. "I don't want to keep you out too late. Not with your coronation tomorrow."

"Fine," Nolia relented, her fingers slipping to his shoulders. "Will you dance with me for one more song?"

Mikael took one of her hands, twirling her before replying with a grin, "Perhaps two if you kiss me again."

25

Audrie

FOR THE CORONATION, Audrie chose to wear white. It wasn't her favorite color to wear, but it was Nolia's, and she wasn't allowed to wear it. She had to wear a shade of purple, the official color of the Icarian royal family.

Audrie thought that she may appreciate the gesture—and was prepared to let Nolia steal it after. The skirt made of feathers was a bit of an extreme, in her opinion, but Cecily had cooed over how beautiful it was. Levi had also said he'd liked it, and Josip had grumbled about how grown up it made her look before interrogating her about the coronation.

"I want to hear every detail," Josip said before they left. "Including how many people they manage to squish into the throne room."

No one bothered to mention that the coronation wasn't being held in the throne room. Nolia had decided that she wanted to have it in the Temple of the Gods.

The temple had been built to honor all fifteen of their gods, but the four major ones were those whose images and symbols were shown. Each wall was dedicated to one of the four. On the left was the wall dedicated to Keyne where the choir was, to the right was Tierra's, in front where the altar stood was Uri's, and the back wall was Mirah's. Hers looked bare compared to the others that were decorated with tapestries and paintings. Audrie assumed that it was due to the decorations all having been gifts from Eteri, Midori, and Kalama; Aecoria certainly wouldn't have sent Icaria many gifts the past couple of years.

Cecily hadn't seemed all that confident when they first entered the temple, but she shrunk further into herself when the guard who'd checked their names off a list led them to the front pew on the left.

"Are you certain?" she asked. "This is a place of honor, for the family of—"

"This is where you were placed," the guard interrupted. "Now if you don't mind, I need to help others find their seats."

Audrie stepped into the pew first, taking the spot directly next to the aisle. She didn't care that her family had to get around her; she wanted to be as close to Nolia as she could be.

As they settled in—Cecily looking incredibly uncomfortable between her children—more guests arrived to fill the front pews. Multiple families filed into the pew across from theirs, and another shuffled into the Girards'.

Cecily stiffened, and Levi took her hand, whispering, "At least we're not here alone."

Audrie was about to agree when she realized who the family belonged to.

"Mikael," Audrie called to him.

Mikael glanced up at her, smiling brightly as he swung a small girl into his arms before going to sit next to Levi. "Audrie," he said. "Levi, Ms. Girard, this is my family."

Mikael began to introduce them, but the only ones whose names Audrie was able to remember were that of his parents: Jibril and Liyana. He had six other sisters aside from Cilia and Rianne, and two of them were married.

Audrie sincerely hoped that she wouldn't need to know their names.

"It's nice to meet you all," she said. "I suppose I should have assumed that you would be invited after everything Mikael has done for Nolia."

"We're quite proud of our son," Liyana agreed, her small silver eyes gazing at Mikael affectionately.

"We don't visit court very often, but a personal invitation from the queen is hard to turn down," Jibril said, smoothing his long black hair down into the neat ponytail he'd arranged it in. He smiled, and while he had darker skin than his son and brown eyes, Audrie could see some of the family resemblance.

"I never thought I'd get to see the palace unless Rianne invited me," said one of Mikael's sisters—Nisiana, Audrie thought her name was. "Turns out that wasn't necessary now that Mikael's one of the queen's favorites."

"Enough to marry one of her ladies," one of the married ones —Lidia?—added.

"They're not engaged," Cilia objected.

The sisters began to bicker, and Audrie stopped trying to follow the conversation. She was certain Mikael was used to the chaos that came with having such a large family, but she wasn't. It had always been her and Levi with their parents—and sometimes Alaric.

Audrie's eyes began to wander as she watched how the other noble families interacted, some sitting far apart silently, others squished together but not talking, while others were chattering away from wherever they sat.

The families in the pew across from Audrie's were a combination of the three, and she assumed that they must have been Nolia's uncles, aunts, and cousins. She was proven correct when she spotted Isidore among them.

Isidore was quiet, staring at the altar and the display table next to it with the objects for the coronation. If Audrie hadn't been wondering about Isiris' whereabouts, she likely would have been more curious about why the crown wasn't being carried in.

Before Audrie could ask Levi or Mikael if they knew, the musicians began to play and the temple's doors opened. Agnesia stepped out, her head high and a solemn smile on her lips as she walked down the aisle.

Isiris strode in behind her, wearing a tight sparkling gown and a baby in a dark purple dress in her arms. People began to whisper as they caught sight of her, some of the older nobles recognizing her. Isiris paid them no mind, reaching the end of the aisle before bowing and going to sit next to her son.

The next people in the procession were two young men who held a large purple carpet in their arms. They set it on the floor before beginning to roll it out backwards so that they wouldn't step on it. Once they reached the front of the aisle, they turned to bow to the altar before taking their seats in the pew across from Audrie's family.

They must be Nolia's cousins, Audrie realized. Which ones, she wasn't sure, but she knew Nolia had five first cousins—at least before Katiana's birth.

One of the boys noticed her staring and winked, making Audrie's face burn from embarrassment.

Fortunately that was when Nolia decided to make her grand entrance.

Nolia's gown was a deep violet with a satin circle skirt and off-the-shoulder straps. Purple magnolia flowers had been embroidered into the bodice in a triangle shape. Where the skirt began was its tip while the flowers decorated her chest and straps.

Nolia's hair was loose, its windswept curls falling down her back as she stepped down the aisle. Her bare feet peeked out from the skirt to reveal purple toenails that Audrie couldn't help but smile at.

When Nolia reached the end of the carpet, she stepped onto the platform's stairs and kneeled before prostrating herself. Audrie winced at how uncomfortable it looked.

"Please sit," Agnesia told the audience as the hymn ended, and Nolia straightened.

ANDREA B. MOLINAR

Everyone did, and Audrie wondered where Nolia would sit since there wasn't a chair for her. But her best friend remained kneeling, so she assumed that was how she'd be stuck the entire ceremony.

Her poor knees, Audrie thought.

"Many years ago, there was a being named Candice, who gave birth to four children," Agnesia began, "Tierra, Keyne, Uri, and Mirah." She pointed to their corresponding walls as she spoke their names. "They were powerful beings like she was, but were discontent alone in their realm—as she had once been. First Candice thought to make them spouses, and started first with Uri's, the most passionate of her children." Agnesia pointed at the ceiling. "She made Amaris out of the essence of her children, but her power had its limits, and she was unable to replicate her success. So she came up with another idea: humans."

Audrie was tempted to sink into her seat. She doubted that there wasn't anyone in the room who didn't already know the story of how their world had come to be. But still Agnesia continued.

"Candice realized that her children together had the unique gifts to craft another realm. So she instructed Keyne to make the sky while Mirah brought the sea into being, with Uri and Amaris becoming what separated night and day, and finally Tierra, constructing the land."

Audrie stifled a yawn.

"Then Candice created humans for her children to interact with and be worshiped by. All was well for a time, but her children grew unsatisfied again and began to quarrel over who had the love of the humans. The humans copied them, taking the side of their favorite god, before lines were drawn and countries dedicated to each god were established."

Almost done, Audrie thought, but she was growing impatient.

"Candice was distressed when she saw the fighting amongst her children and that of the humans who adored them. So she made the decision to create another country, Icaria, who would not worship her or one other god, but all of them. She asked Tierra to build

240

an island nearby, before populating it with the humans from the five original countries. From among them, she picked the first Riona queen, who she gave the largest responsibility any human has ever had: to keep Icaria flourishing and at peace, so the rest of the world would also be."

Audrie almost let out a breath of relief now that she'd finally reached the end of the story. She just wanted to see Nolia crowned and eat her heart out at the feast; she'd been fasting all day to have space in her stomach.

"Please stand, Nolia, and face your people," Agnesia said.

Nolia did so, turning around to stare out at the crowd, but Audrie could tell she wasn't really looking at any of them. Her royal blue eyes showed that her mind was elsewhere. Likely on the vows she was about to make.

The musicians played another hymn as Isiris stood again with baby Katiana, going to the display table that Agnesia was next to. She handed Katiana over to her—making Audrie wonder why she'd brought the baby in the first place—before picking up the scepter, sword, and purple ermine-trimmed robe.

They were arranged carefully in Isiris' arms as she went to Nolia, bowing her head as Nolia took them from her.

First was the robe, which she tied loosely around her neck and made sure her hair wasn't stuck under before she took the scepter in her right hand and the sword in her left.

Agnesia scooped up the crown next, handing it and Katiana to Isiris before placing herself on Nolia's right, across from Isiris, as the music came to an end.

"Nolia Riona, daughter and heir of Queen Katrine," Agnesia said, "from the time of your birth, you were raised to be Icaria's next queen. Are you ready and willing to take the throne?"

"I am." Nolia's voice didn't waver, and Audrie swelled with pride.

Agnesia smiled before beginning the vows. "Do you, Nolia Riona, promise to rule justly and do what is in the best interest of the Icarian people?"

Audrie's heart was beating so loudly in her ears that she almost didn't hear Nolia say, "I do."

Agnesia continued, "Do you, Nolia Riona, promise to keep the gods with you in all that you do as queen and strive to lead our country spiritually?"

Nolia nodded. "I do."

"Do you, Nolia Riona, promise to maintain the peace within Icaria as Candice has instructed every Riona queen before you to do?"

Nolia's hands tightened around the sword and scepter, making her knuckles turn white before she answered, "I do."

Agnesia turned towards the pews, her eyes bright with excitement. "Icarian subjects, do you accept Nolia Riona as your queen and welcome her onto your throne?"

"We do!" everyone shouted, Audrie loudest of all.

Nolia's eyes flicked to hers, the amusement mixing with her relief.

"I introduce to you, Nolia Riona, Queen of Icaria!" Agnesia bellowed as Isiris placed the crown on Nolia's head.

The crowd kneeled, and the musicians played a hymn that Audrie knew, the one praising Candice for the existence of their strong line of Rionas. Everyone's heads were bowed save for Audrie's, and that of Nolia's cousins' children and Mikael's little sisters, who were throwing magnolia flowers from their seats towards her.

Nolia grinned at the children, but most of all at Audrie, before she set down the scepter and sword, and untied the robe to return it all to the table. She waited for the music to end for everyone to stand and stare back at their newly crowned queen.

"Good Icarian people," Nolia said, "I thank you for being with me on this momentous day. Before we feast, there's something I would like to do first."

Excited murmurs broke out around Audrie, curiosity coating the air so thickly that she nearly jumped when she heard her name.

"Audrie Girard." Nolia reached her hand out to her. "Join me?"

The noble's voices disappeared then, and Audrie didn't feel her legs move. All she saw was Nolia, her best friend as the beautiful queen she was always meant to be, using her first act as a crowned monarch for *her*.

Audrie took Nolia's hand before she kneeled as she instructed her.

"Audrie, you have been my best friend from the time we were children." Nolia smiled down at her. "You have been my closest confidante, the person who understands me best, and most importantly, my savior. I would not be alive today if you had not saved me from Elias' attack in the tower."

The crowd gasped, and Audrie almost rolled her eyes since surely they knew he was behind all of that, but she kept her gaze on Nolia.

Nolia turned back to the display table, gingerly lifting the sword with two hands before looking at Audrie again. "No queen has ever had a protector and friend as true as you are, so that's why I'm going to give you a title that no one has ever given." Nolia tapped Audrie's shoulders gently. "Audrie Girard, daughter of Cecily, I name you the Knight of Icaria."

• • •

The end of the coronation was a blur. Audrie remembered watching Nolia glide down the aisle, the music blaring in her ears, before the carpet was rolled back up, and Isiris left with Katiana. Nolia's family went after them, and Agnesia told Audrie to go as well.

So she did. The nobles stared at her with bewildered eyes, but Audrie hardly noticed. She was too eager to get to Nolia again—whether it was to thank her for her new title or confront her about not warning her beforehand.

But when Audrie got outside of the temple, Nolia had already been whisked away, so she waited for her family on the temple's left side as the guests exited.

"My lady, you look as if you're in need of an escort."

It took Audrie a moment to realize that the voice was talking to her, and she looked up, seeing the boy that had winked at her.

"You're Nolia's cousin," she blurted out.

"I am." He smiled crookedly at her. "I'm Cathrinus, I'm sure she's mentioned me before."

"I'm sure she has," Audrie agreed, glancing towards the doors to see if her family had escaped the temple yet.

"Your family will make their way towards the ballroom eventually," Cathrinus said, clearly knowing what she was thinking. "Would you allow me to take you there?"

Audrie bit her lip, debating whether or not to continue waiting for Levi and Cecily. The nobles weren't pouring out very quickly; they evidently weren't as hungry as Audrie was.

"Icaria's Knight already has an escort."

The new voice made Audrie's heart jump, but she somehow kept her face from showing it.

Darius wasn't nearly as good at hiding his emotions, scowling at Cathrinus as he appeared at her side.

"My apologies, I had no idea," Cathrinus replied, giving Darius a tense smile before bowing to Audrie. "Perhaps you'll save me a dance for later, my lady? If only to thank you for saving my cousin's life."

"Of course," Audrie said, and he winked again before disappearing into the crowd.

Darius moved to her side, but when it became apparent that he had no intention of speaking, Audrie crossed her arms.

"You had no right to chase him off," she said.

"Don't tell me you were interested in him," Darius answered. "He's just some pompous prince who's only interested in the benefits your new title will grant you."

Audrie rolled her eyes. "He looked at me before I was granted my new title, but thanks for the warning."

"He looked at you?" Darius said dryly. "He must already be in love."

"You know what I meant."

Darius didn't reply, and Audrie studied him, in his black pants and coat that he was rather handsome in. When he met her eyes, she quickly said, "Jealousy isn't a very good look on you."

"Who said I was jealous?" Darius snapped back.

"Don't pretend you aren't," Audrie told him.

Darius' face grew red, and for a moment, Audrie thought he was going to fling an insult at her. Instead he answered, "So what if I was?"

Audrie blinked at him. "You're being honest with me for once?"

"For once?" Darius repeated. "I've always been honest with you. You're the one who pretended to be a boy when you weren't."

You weren't honest about your feelings for me or Rubin, Audrie thought, but she supposed that wasn't fair. She'd never specifically asked him about either.

"What happened with Rubin?"

Darius sighed. "Why do you always have to bring him up?"

"Because he's your boyfriend..." Audrie paused. "Or he was."

"We never called each other that, but he was in a way," Darius agreed. "Now he isn't."

"But why?" Audrie insisted, thinking of the way the boys had greeted each other days before. "Don't you care about him? After everything that's happened, why—"

"It's because of everything that's happened that I let him go," Darius interrupted. "Rubin should have never come to the Competition or fought the rebels, but he did for me. He's loyal to me in a way that I never could be." Darius swallowed before adding in a low tone, "At least not to him. I wouldn't have gambled my life so many times with rebels and attempted royal murders for Rubin. But I did for you, with the knowledge that I may never get anything out of it, because it was *you* who needed me. I couldn't possibly remain with him after that."

It struck Audrie odd how Darius' mind worked. He showed no remorse for killing or violence, but he did for Rubin. It shouldn't have been as heartwarming as it was.

"I think I may like you after all." Audrie stepped closer to him. "Despite your many, many flaws."

"I know I like you," Darius replied, reaching for her waist. "Particularly when you're not asking me to risk my life."

"Really?" Audrie rested her hands on his chest. "You seem to want to kiss me when I am."

"I want to kiss you all the more when you aren't," Darius answered, his violet eyes bright. "Like right now."

They stared at each other, the moment stretching for only a breath before Audrie took his face in her hands, and his lips eagerly met hers. Darius brought her closer to him, pressing their bodies together and sending a thrill through Audrie.

She pulled away, smiling at him, and Darius looked ready to kiss her again when someone cleared their throat.

"Levi." Audrie spotted her brother, her face growing warm, but she wasn't nearly as embarrassed as she thought she'd be.

Levi rolled his eyes. "I don't want to hear anything about Lia and me ever again."

Audrie let go of Darius. "You're still interested in her?" she asked. "Even though she's Elias' spy?"

Levi motioned towards Darius. "You're still interested in him? Even though—"

"Actually Lia *was* his spy," Darius interrupted, clearly not wanting to hear the end of his sentence; not that Audrie did either. He ran a hand through his hair as if trying to fix it, although Audrie hadn't touched it, before adding, "It makes sense now why Audrie was so eager to change that."

Levi sighed. "Let's go to the feast," he said. "And no more kissing. At least not in front of me."

"Of course not," Darius agreed, and when Levi turned around, he pressed his lips to Audrie's again.

"What—?" she began, but he quieted her with a smirk and a whisper.

"It wasn't in front of him."

26

Nolia

THE FEAST, LIKE the coronation, had been hastily put together. Nolia hadn't had the time or energy to decide on a specific theme or pick out dishes. Fortunately, the servants hadn't gotten rid of the decorations they'd been meaning to use during her engagement celebrations, and the cooks knew her favorite foods. It all came together quite nicely, in her opinion.

Fresh magnolias hung from the ceiling, having been picked and sewn together by the staff with great care. They were strung with crystal lights that lit up the room, allowing the guests to see the pristinely white tablecloths they ate on top of. There were also tall gold candlesticks on the tables that matched the platters the courses were brought out in, and the gold detailing of the porcelain plates they would eat off of. Each chair was sufficiently cushioned and had a string of pearls, except for Nolia's that had a large purple bow.

The tables had been arranged in a large rectangle shape with Nolia's platformed one for her and her family at its head so that everyone would have a perfect view of Nolia, regardless of whether she was seated or on the dance floor.

Nolia danced first with her uncles, and it made her wonder if Elias was supposed to have been the first person she danced with. The thought sent chills running down her back, and she was glad when she moved onto her cousins afterwards. She danced with the five of them based on their birth order, and when she got to Caius, Nolia relaxed, thinking she would be done dancing for the time being.

Until the song ended, and Nolia realized there was someone else waiting for her at the edge of the dance floor.

Audrie beamed at her, arms crossed over the lovely white gown she wore, and Nolia abandoned her cousin before the last note of the song to go to her.

"Your Majesty." Audrie curtsied before offering Nolia her hands. "Would you do me the honor of a dance?"

Nolia gripped her hands. "Always."

Before Audrie could pull her back onto the dance floor, Nolia turned towards the rest of the guests. "My first decree as a crowned queen," she began, over their murmurs, "is that you all find yourselves a dance partner and join me in dancing the night away."

She nodded to the musicians, and they began another song. Nobles rushed out of their seats, surrounding the best friends, but the girls hardly noticed.

Audrie spun them in a circle, and Nolia was reminded again of their pretend balls. Back then they'd argued about who would play the princess and who the prince. If only their younger selves could see them now with no prince necessary.

Audrie looked as if she knew what she was thinking before giving her an awkward smile. "I've been meaning to talk to you about Mikael," she said.

"I've been meaning to talk to you about Darius," Nolia responded.

Audrie gave her a teasing smile, but it slipped, becoming more serious. "So you know about Mikael?"

"And he knows about how I feel too." Nolia spotted him at one of the longer tables where they'd somehow managed to squish his large family. He was caught up in conversation with Rianne, but he seemed to feel her eyes on his, and he swiftly met her gaze. The grin he gave her had Nolia promising herself that she'd dance with him again that night, regardless of who was watching.

Audrie's eyes widened. "You and Mikael—?"

"Have you and Darius figured things out yet?" Nolia interrupted. "He's certainly staring at you like you have."

Nolia had given him a seat at the Girard's table, next to where Mikael and his family were. He was ignoring the conversation going on around him, his attention solely on Audrie.

Audrie smirked in his direction, but there was a hint of blush on her cheeks. "Yes."

"Good." Nolia's heart swelled at the joy shining in her best friend's eyes, one that she knew was mirroring her own.

"Let's go," Audrie said as the song came to an end. "There's somewhere else we should be."

Nolia raised her eyebrows at her. "Other than my coronation ball?"

"Yes." Audrie squeezed her hands. "Trust me."

• • •

Nolia never knew what to expect when it came to surprises from Audrie, but she hadn't thought that she would bring her to a grave.

"They buried her here." Nolia kneeled in front of it, gently touching the engraving of the small plaque that was hardly visible in the darkness of the garden. "They didn't send her body back to Espin."

Her guards shifted restlessly behind her and Audrie, but she ignored them. They hadn't wanted her to go, claiming it would be dangerous, but Audrie had insisted it was for good reason.

"Your mother must have known you'd want her nearby," Audrie said.

Nolia didn't find that likely, but she didn't say so. Katrine had naturally had a governess too, and she'd still been alive when Nolia was born. She had enough memories of her and Katrine to feel that they'd never been close as Nolia and Corinne had been.

"She died for me," Nolia said instead. "Perhaps that's why she thought Corinne was deserving of such an honorable resting place."

ANDREA B. MOLINAR

Audrie set a hand on her shoulder. "I'm sorry I didn't bring you sooner," she said. "But now felt like the right moment."

"It is," Nolia agreed. "She should have been part of this night."

"Now she is." Audrie let out a small laugh. "Although you know what feels ironic? Corinne's resting place is closer to you than Katrine's is. It's kind of like how it was in life. She was always the one nearby, not your mother."

"They were both my mothers in different ways," Nolia answered, sighing before standing. She hoped that once she got into the light, she'd see that she hadn't gotten her gown dirty. The seamstresses who had rushed to make it certainly wouldn't be pleased if it were.

"Now you'll always have both of your mothers nearby."

Nolia turned to look at Audrie. "Yours won't be all that far away either. Your father too."

Unlike mine, she added to herself. Elias' body had already been cremated, and she hadn't asked where his ashes would be strewn. She'd let Isiris take care of that, and knowing her, she'd probably dump them in the sea. It was a good place for someone who'd been accidentally working with Aecoria.

"I don't know if I'll ever forgive him, but I hope he and my mother are happier this time," Audrie said. "That's all I want to say about that."

Nolia nodded, hooking an arm through hers. "What do you want to talk about then? More about how good of a kisser Darius is?"

"Only if you want to talk about Mikael's lips," Audrie replied.

The best friends stuck their tongues out at each other before taking their time going back to Candicia. The guards grumbled behind them.

"I think I'd rather talk about you and me," Audrie said.

"What about us?"

"How things are going to be different," Audrie responded. "Your father and Justina are gone, so most of Icaria's rebels are too.

You have an almost-fiancé and a queendom to maintain lasting peace in. Plus you must be worried about this mysterious Moselle."

They took a couple of steps before Nolia spoke. "I'm not worried about her," she admitted. "I have a feeling that there is no Moselle, and even if she does exist, Mirah doesn't want her to have Icaria."

Audrie stared at her. "You can't possibly know that."

Nolia shrugged. "I can't explain how it is I know. I just do."

And Nolia did. The sense of peace that she felt at the thought of Aecoria's mysterious queen was almost terrifying. But she knew that Mirah meant her no harm, and never would.

"Fine," Audrie said as they neared the palace doors. "What about everything else? How is it going to affect you and me?"

"I don't know why you think they have to change anything between us."

"You're queen with a new boyfriend you don't have to hide from anyone," Audrie said, not saying the last part as quietly as Nolia would have liked. "There's no crisis that you'll ask my help with. You won't need me anymore, so where does that leave things between us?"

The girls paused as the guards opened the doors to let them inside, and the chandelier in the hallway lit up their faces. Nolia could see now the pink flush on Audrie's cheeks and the way her golden flecked brown eyes glinted with worry.

"As best friends," Nolia told her. "The queen and her knight."

"Except that 'Knight of Icaria' is an entirely made-up title," Audrie said, her lips twitching into a smile.

"It's not just a title, it's an incredibly important position to have," Nolia replied.

"So it's a position now?" Audrie said, raising her eyebrows. "What does it entail? Training with the army? Becoming a commander? Being the head of your armies?"

The guards grumbled louder at that, and Nolia grinned, keeping her eyes on her best friend. "It can if you want," she said, stopping them in the middle of the hallway. "All that I was thinking about when I made you my knight is that it would mean we would never be separated. No Competitions or rebels or anything worse will take us away from each other ever again."

Audrie fully smiled then, her relief washing over into Nolia too. "That sounds better than perfect to me."

Audrie and Nolia's story may have come to an end...
but Seraphina Moselle's is only just beginning.

SERAPHINA
OF THE SUN

COMING MAY 2025

Through the battle
Of a daughter of the sun and a daughter of the sea
Will Uri and Mirah's eternal war unravel.

By the champion's hand, it will be
The fall of the sun
Or a drought for the sea.

The victorious daughter alone will decide
Which god shall forever more preside.

GLOSSARY OF THE GODS

Candice
The Mother of the Gods
Country: Icaria

The Main Gods
Tierra
Goddess of the Earth and
Agriculture
Country: Midori

Keyne
God of the Sky and Air
Country: Eteri

Uri
God of the Sun and Fire
Country: Kalama

Mirah
Goddess of the Sea and
Water
Country: Aecoria

The Minor Gods
Children of Tierra
Kalila
Goddess of Love and
Marriage
Country: Erastus

Irina
Goddess of Peace
Country: Concordia

Galina
Goddess of Medicine and
Childbearing
Country: Bliant

Children of Keyne

Omeir
God of Time
Country: Horatia

Nuncio
God of Prophecy and
Fortune
Country: Bedisa

Synan
God of Wisdom and
Knowledge
Country: Monisha

Family of Uri

Amaris
Goddess of the Moon (and
Uri's wife)
Country: Chandra

Azrail
God of the Afterlife
Country: Kalid

Reverie
Goddess of Sleep and
Dreams
Country: Rasui

Children of Mirah

Alzena
Goddess of the Arts
Country: Cetaka

Seraphina Moselle

Cadoc
God of War
Country: Agrona

ACKNOWLEDGEMENTS

Finishing a book series is only something I've done a handful of times before now, but the Icaria Trilogy may be the one I'm proudest of (seeing as how this is my first published series and all).

Thank you to my fantastic editor, Cara, for putting so much into *Queenly* and my writing. Your help and encouragement has been amazing, and I sincerely look forward to continuing to work with you.

Thank you to Tania and my cover art team at Mibl Art for another wonderful cover. You somehow make my terrible sketches into a reality that isn't terrible at all.

Thank you to my family. To my parents for your support as I continue to work towards my dreams. To Jesse for not letting it get to your head that a book was dedicated to you. To Penny and Toby for never being far while I'm busy typing away.

Thank you to all of the friends and family who have been with me on this journey. From those of you who've attended my book signings to those who've posted about my books on social media and told everyone who would listen.

Finally, thank you to you. Yes, YOU. Words can't express how grateful I am to you for taking a chance on my series and reading it to the end. I hope you'll join me for the next one too.

Andrea B. Molinar is the author of the Icaria Trilogy. She grew up in Northern California where she wrote her first story at age seven and hasn't stopped writing since. She studied journalism and creative writing at Sacramento State University, and wrote the first draft of her debut *Knightly* before graduating in 2022. When she's not writing, Andrea can be found reading, dancing, or daydreaming about her characters' next adventure.

Find Andrea on:
Website: andreabmolinar17.wixsite.com/andreabmolinar
Instagram: @andreabmolinar
TikTok: @andreabmolinar

Made in the USA
Monee, IL
12 October 2024

67141046R00156